Late Night Meetings

Assisting the Boss Series, Volume 3

Lexy Timms

Published by Dark Shadow Publishing, 2020.

This is a work of fiction. Similarities to real people, places, or events are entirely coincidental.

LATE NIGHT MEETINGS

First edition. April 1, 2020.

Copyright © 2020 Lexy Timms.

Written by Lexy Timms.

Also by Lexy Timms

A Bad Boy Bullied Romance
I Hate You
I Hate You A Little Bit
I Hate You A Little Bit More

A Burning Love Series
Spark of Passion
Flame of Desire
Blaze of Ecstasy

A Chance at Forever Series
Forever Perfect
Forever Desired
Forever Together

A Dating App Series
I've Been Matched
You've Been Matched

We've Been Matched

A "Kind of" Billionaire
Taking a Risk
Safety in Numbers
Pretend You're Mine

A Maybe Series
Maybe I Should
Maybe I Shouldn't
Maybe I Did

Assisting the Boss Series
Billion Reasons
Duke of Delegation
Late Night Meetings
Delegating Love

BBW Romance Series
Capturing Her Beauty
Pursuing Her Dreams
Tracing Her Curves

Beating the Biker Series

Making Her His
Making the Break
Making of Them

Billionaire Banker Series
Banking on Him
Price of Passion
Investing in Love
Knowing Your Worth
Treasured Forever
Banking on Christmas

Billionaire Holiday Romance Series
Driving Home for Christmas
The Valentine Getaway
Cruising Love

Billionaire in Disguise Series
Facade
Illusion
Charade

Billionaire Secrets Series
The Secret
Freedom
Courage

Trust
Impulse
Billionaire Secrets Box Set Books #1-3

Blind Sight Series
See Me
Fix Me
Eyes On Me

Branded Series
Money or Nothing
What People Say
Give and Take

Building Billions
Building Billions - Part 1
Building Billions - Part 2
Building Billions - Part 3

Change of Heart Series
The Heart Needs
The Heart Wants
The Heart Knows

Faking It
Temporary CEO
Caught in the Act
Never Tell A Lie
Fake Christmas
Fake Billionaire Box Set #1-3

Firehouse Romance Series
Caught in Flames
Burning With Desire
Craving the Heat
Firehouse Romance Complete Collection

Forging Billions Series
Dirty Money
Petty Cash
Payment Required

For His Pleasure
Elizabeth
Georgia
Madison

Fortune Riders MC Series
Billionaire Biker
Billionaire Ransom

Billionaire Misery

Fragile Series
Fragile Touch
Fragile Kiss
Fragile Love

Great Temptation Series
The Devil's Footsteps
Heaven's Command
Mortals Surrender

Hades' Spawn Motorcycle Club
One You Can't Forget
One That Got Away
One That Came Back
One You Never Leave
One Christmas Night
Hades' Spawn MC Complete Series

Hard Rocked Series
Rhyme
Harmony
Lyrics

Heart of Stone Series
The Protector
The Guardian
The Warrior

Heart of the Battle Series
Celtic Viking
Celtic Rune
Celtic Mann
Heart of the Battle Series Box Set

Heistdom Series
Master Thief
Goldmine
Diamond Heist
Smile For Me
Your Move
Green With Envy
Saving Money

Highlander Wolf Series
Pack Run
Pack Land
Pack Rules

Discord
Tenacity

Love on the Sea Series
Ships Ahoy

Love You Series
Love Life
Need Love
My Love

Managing the Billionaire
Never Enough
Worth the Cost
Secret Admirers
Chasing Affection
Pressing Romance
Timeless Memories
The Night Before Christmas

Managing the Bosses Series
The Boss
The Boss Too
Who's the Boss Now
Love the Boss
I Do the Boss

Wife to the Boss
Employed by the Boss
Brother to the Boss
Senior Advisor to the Boss
Forever the Boss
Christmas With the Boss
Billionaire in Control
Billionaire Makes Millions
Billionaire at Work
Precious Little Thing
Priceless Love
Valentine Love
The Cost of Freedom
Trick or Treat
Gift for the Boss - Novella 3.5
Managing the Bosses Box Set #1-3
Managing the Bosses Novellas

Model Mayhem Series
Shameless
Modesty
Imperfection

Moment in Time
Highlander's Bride
Victorian Bride
Modern Day Bride
A Royal Bride
Forever the Bride

My Best Friend's Sister
Hometown Calling
A Perfect Moment
Thrown in Together

My Darker Side Series
Darkest Hour
Time to Stop
Against the Light

Neverending Dream Series
Neverending Dream - Part 1
Neverending Dream - Part 2
Neverending Dream - Part 3
Neverending Dream - Part 4
Neverending Dream - Part 5

Outside the Octagon
Submit
Fight
Knockout

Protecting Diana Series
Her Bodyguard

Her Defender
Her Champion
Her Protector
Her Forever

Protecting Layla Series
His Mission
His Objective
His Devotion

Racing Hearts Series
Rush
Pace
Fast

Regency Romance Series
The Duchess Scandal - Part 1
The Duchess Scandal - Part 2

Reverse Harem Series
Primals
Archaic
Unitary

RIP Series
Track the Ripper
Hunt the Ripper
Pursue the Ripper

R&S Rich and Single Series
Alex Reid
Parker

Saving Forever
Saving Forever - Part 1
Saving Forever - Part 2
Saving Forever - Part 3
Saving Forever - Part 4
Saving Forever - Part 5
Saving Forever - Part 6
Saving Forever Part 7
Saving Forever - Part 8
Saving Forever Boxset Books #1-3

Shifting Desires Series
Jungle Heat
Jungle Fever
Jungle Blaze

Sin Series
Payment for Sin
Atonement Within
Declaration of Love

Southern Romance Series
Little Love Affair
Siege of the Heart
Freedom Forever
Soldier's Fortune

Spanked Series
Passion
Playmate
Pleasure

Spelling Love Series
The Author
The Book Boyfriend
The Words of Love

Taboo Wedding Series
He Loves Me Not
With This Ring

Happily Ever After

Tattooist Series
Confession of a Tattooist
Surrender of a Tattooist
Heart of a Tattooist
Hopes & Dreams of a Tattooist

Tennessee Romance
Whisky Lullaby
Whisky Melody
Whisky Harmony

The Bad Boy Alpha Club
Battle Lines - Part 1
Battle Lines

The Brush Of Love Series
Every Night
Every Day
Every Time
Every Way
Every Touch

The Debt
The Debt: Part 1 - Damn Horse
The Debt: Complete Collection

The Fire Inside Series
Dare Me
Defy Me
Burn Me

The Gentleman's Club Series
Gambler
Player
Wager

The Golden Mail
Hot Off the Press
Extra! Extra!
Read All About It
Stop the Press
Breaking News
This Just In

The Lucky Billionaire Series
Lucky Break

Streak of Luck
Lucky in Love

The Sound of Breaking Hearts Series
Disruption
Destroy
Devoted

The University of Gatica Series
The Recruiting Trip
Faster
Higher
Stronger
Dominate
No Rush
University of Gatica - The Complete Series

T.N.T. Series
Troubled Nate Thomas - Part 1
Troubled Nate Thomas - Part 2
Troubled Nate Thomas - Part 3

Toxic Touch Series
Noxious

Undercover Series
Perfect For Me
Perfect For You
Perfect For Us

Unknown Identity Series
Unknown
Unpublished
Unexposed
Unsure
Unwritten
Unknown Identity Box Set: Books #1-3

Unlucky Series
Unlucky in Love
UnWanted
UnLoved Forever

War Torn Letters Series
My Sweetheart
My Darling
My Beloved

Wet & Wild Series

Stormy Love
Savage Love
Secure Love

Worth It Series
Worth Billions
Worth Every Cent
Worth More Than Money

You & Me - A Bad Boy Romance
Just Me
Touch Me
Kiss Me

Standalone
Wash
Loving Charity
Summer Lovin'
Love & College
Billionaire Heart
First Love
Frisky and Fun Romance Box Collection
Beating Hades' Bikers

Watch for more at www.lexytimms.com.

Late Night MEETINGS

ASSISTING THE *Boss* SERIES

USA TODAY BESTSELLING AUTHOR

LEXY TIMMS

Copyright 2020

———— ● ————

All rights reserved.
Late Night Meetings
Assisting the Boss Series #3
Copyright 2020 by Lexy Timms
Cover by: Book Cover by Design[1]

---

1. http://bookcoverbydesign.co.uk/

Assisting the Boss Series

Want to read more...
For **FREE?**
Sign up for Lexy Timms' newsletter
And she'll send you updates on new releases, ARC copies of books
and a whole lotta fun!
Sign up for news and updates!
http://eepurl.com/9i0vD

Late Night Meetings Blurb:

BEST MOMENTS HAPPEN when they are unplanned.

Back to New York. Back to reality. But that trip to California has changed everything—and we both know it.

I just want to forget Lilah and move on with my life, but the world isn't making that easy. My mother won't get off my back about bringing her into the fold again. And the stress at work is piling up without her smile to take the edge off. And she was damn good at her job. I can't lie about that.

But she's not waiting around for me. And I'm not sure how much more of not being able to have her that I can take...

Chapter One

Lilah

"ALL RIGHT, ALL RIGHT, all right," Violet told me, raising her hand to stop me in my tracks. "Start from the beginning again. What happened?"

Sighing heavily, I sank my head back on to the couch. I couldn't believe that any of this had actually happened. I couldn't believe I had been stupid enough to fall for it.

I should have known better. I should have known better than to fly off on that trip with him and act like it wasn't going to lead to anything else. I had known from the moment we took off that something was going to happen, and I hadn't stopped it.

Hell, if anything, I had wanted it. I had needed his touch, his attention, everything he had lavished on me that first time we had gone away together.

But now, it was over. It was over and done with and I had been the one to put the final nail in the coffin of everything that had been happening between us. I knew it was for the best really, but that didn't make it any easier to handle.

He had just been so fucking confusing. And I needed someone in my life who could make things easier to understand, not drive me crazy as I tried to wrap my head around just what he intended for me.

"So, when you got there, everything was normal?" Violet asked.

I sighed and nodded, then launched into the story from the start once more. I had come through the door and basically shouted bits of it at her from my bedroom as I tossed around all my clothes and put them back in their place, but she hadn't been able to piece much together.

So I ran through everything again from the beginning. The trip, the sex, the movies, the romance, and then him turning on me like none of that had happened in the first place, making me feel like it had been a mistake from the start.

I should have known better than to fall into bed with him again. I should have been more careful. Hell, I knew that much for sure, even though I had been all too eager to just slide into bed with him the very first chance I got. The reality was I loved being around him, and there was something about the attitude he took on outside of work that made me feel as though he wanted me, as though it was about more than just the way I looked and instead had everything to do with the way that I made him feel.

And maybe that was the truth. Or maybe I had just convinced myself of that because I couldn't resist his touch once again. I had no idea, and looking back wasn't making it any clearer to me. Well, until Violet said the very last thing on earth that I wanted to hear.

"So you were the one who said you wanted to keep it professional?"

I nodded. "Yeah, I did."

I knew that I was a hypocrite of the highest order and that I had a hell of a lot to answer for, given all the rules that I had laid out and then turned my back on as soon as the opportunity arose. I was a fucking idiot really, and I knew it. But that didn't mean that I felt any better about what had happened between us.

We were supposed to just go golfing. Nothing more than that. I had been the one to make that clear, and he would have gone along with it, too. I knew that he would. If I'd asked, he would have rented out a whole other bungalow for me to stay in so that we didn't have to share a space, if that was what had made me comfortable. But I had gone along with it because, in the back of my mind, whether I wanted to admit it or not, I needed to be close to him in that way.

"And when you guys slept together," she continued. "You wanted more, right?"

"Yeah, I did," I admitted. "I just—we're good together like that. And I thought it might have been the start of something real. I knew that we had some issues with it before, but it felt different then. I was sure that we could find some way to make it work."

"Even though you told him that's not what you wanted," she reminded me.

I winced. "Yeah, even though I told him that," I confessed.

The more she was talking about it, the more I felt like all of this just boiled down to being my fault more than anything else. If I had been a little clearer, if I had laid down the law and made it obvious that this wasn't going to go anywhere else, maybe I wouldn't have taken it so badly when he had spoken to me like that. Maybe—

"You quit, right?" she asked me. "The job, I mean. Not just whatever was happening with him."

"I did."

"So what are you going to do for work now?"

I sank my head into my hands and shrugged my shoulders. "I have no idea what I'm going to do."

I knew I should have thought a little harder about the fact that I had just given up the job. I should have focused a little harder on finding a way to navigate around the awkwardness that I had managed to make happen between us, but I felt like it just wasn't that easy.

I couldn't stand to be around him any longer, not after what had happened between us. Not after knowing that he would still just click back into this form with no warning, that he would still treat me as a throwaway when he got the chance. I needed more than that. I deserved more than that too. I was sure of it.

"I do, though," Violet told me firmly. "First, you need to get some rest. Sounds like you've had one hell of a trip. I thought going on vacation was meant to be relaxing, right?"

"Yeah, something like that," I replied, managing to smile at her.

I got to my feet and stretched my arms over my head. Shit, I felt like I needed to crawl into bed and sleep for twenty years. Which I could actually do now, given that I had just left my job and had no reason to turn up to work again anytime soon.

"Good night, Vi," I murmured to her. "I'll speak to you tomorrow, all right?"

"Sleep as long as you need to," she replied, waving her hand to dismiss me. "Sounds like you have a lot of pieces to put together right now."

I headed through to bed and closed the door behind me. As soon as I heard it click into the latch, I flopped down and let out a groan. I couldn't believe I had let all of that happen to me.

I had promised myself when we arrived back at work after that first trip that this would be different. That I wouldn't just give in to what I wanted and that I would pay attention for a change to what was going on in my head. I needed to make money, I needed to get back on my feet, and I wasn't going to do that by sliding into bed with the man who was meant to be paying my wages at the end of every month.

Honestly, I should have known myself better by now really. I should have known that I had this habit of pushing against the rules I made for myself, even when I knew they were in my best interest. How could I resist a man like that when I knew that I wanted him and knew that I couldn't have him?

It was almost unfair of me to put those rules on myself, and even more unfair of me to expect him to abide by them when I hardly had a handle on them by myself.

But that didn't mean he'd had the right to treat me the way he had. Not a chance in hell. I just didn't understand how he managed to slip from one version of himself to the other so damn quickly, without any space in between for me to make sense of what had just happened.

I deserved at least that much, didn't I? I deserved an explanation as to why he had shifted so suddenly from the version of him that seemed to like me to the one that seemed to want nothing to do with me. It just wasn't fair. I didn't understand how he could change so fast.

And that was what I was angry about more than anything. Yes, sure, I was mad at myself for giving in to him again so quickly, but I was madder at him because he had known that I wanted him. He had known that this was shifting into something new, something different.

He had been the one who had basically initiated all that romance, all that lovey-dovey stuff. Whisking me out for that private picnic, just the two of us, holding my hand when we were out together, making sure that the whole world knew I belonged to him and he wasn't going to let anything change that. It was more than any decent person could handle without falling a little in love, and it was unfair of him to think that he could pull all of that out of the hat and then just go back to normal. Go back to how he always was. Not expecting me to see one drop of difference in all of that.

I missed that version of him. That was the one that I wanted above all else. Not the version that seemed to snap and change as soon as something went wrong. The one that reacted to hearing from his father as though he wanted to flip a table. The one that stormed around and told me to get ready so we could leave with no warning. I didn't want that man. I wanted the one who treated me like he couldn't get enough of me, someone who was sweet, earnest, and kind.

But I knew that I didn't get to pick and choose between versions of him like that. If I wanted him, then I wanted all of him, and it didn't work any other way. I couldn't just decide that I didn't like this part of him, no matter how irritating it seemed or how far removed it was from the man who treated me like I deserved all the care and attention in the world. I had to accept that they all came as part of one package, and that package was what I was signing up for if I wanted to be with him at all.

And that was that. I didn't. I couldn't, not if it meant dealing with him when he snapped at me for no reason.

I wasn't going to put up with being treated that way. Not a chance in hell. I had better things to do with my life than run around trying to make him happy when I knew that it would never really happen.

Yet, there was some part of me—no matter how ill-informed, no matter how naïve—that hoped I would be able to find something else inside of him. What was it they said? That a man sometimes just needed the love of a good woman to draw him out of his state of distrust and distaste. Perhaps that was all he was waiting for really. Perhaps that was all that he needed.

After all, from what he had told me about his parents, it wasn't as though he'd had the best people to base his love life on. His mom and dad had split up when he was young, and his dad had taken off with a collection of wives young enough to be his siblings practically. No wonder he had no faith in the way all of this went. I didn't think I would have been able to mess much of it up, not after what he had been through.

But did that mean that I had to be the one to fix it? No, I couldn't do that for anyone. Let alone a grown man like him.

He was old enough now that he was set in his ways, and if his ways involved turning into an asshole whenever things didn't go his way, then that wasn't my problem to fix.

When I had been his assistant, sure, I needed to help out with the way he lived his life day in and day out. But that didn't mean I had to do the same thing as his girlfriend.

There were men out there who had already come to terms with the people that they were, who weren't going to hold my attitude against me, who were never going to make me feel the way he did. And those were the men I was holding out for.

I had spent enough of my life running around after guys who didn't know how to act like men, and I wasn't about to waste another moment on one who couldn't get his shit together the way I knew he already should have.

I was done with him. I was going to turn in my letter of resignation before he got into work the next day and leave all this behind me once and for all. No looking back. I had to move forward now, and nothing was going to stop me in chasing down whatever came next.

Chapter Two

Damian

MY APARTMENT FELT QUIET.

It always did, and normally, I liked that. I had to be around people all day long, so I liked taking a break and coming back here, knowing that I didn't have to talk to anyone for the rest of the evening if I didn't feel like it.

But after spending those few days with Lilah at the resort in California, I needed noise. Something. Anything that would let me pretend she hadn't just ditched the hell out of me and help me forget that I had no idea if she was coming back.

She acted like she didn't want to return. Fine. If that was how she felt about it, I wasn't going to stand here and make a big deal about getting her back. If she was done with me, there was no way in hell I was going to make a fool of myself by chasing her down and acting like she had any obligation to stick around with me.

The flight home had been long and quiet, and I had tried a couple of times to make conversation with her in the hopes of lightening the mood and maybe breaking down the barriers she had thrown up between the two of us.

"So what do you want to do when you get back?" I'd asked her.

She hadn't taken her eyes off the window. She could have pretended to be asleep if she really didn't want me talking to her, but it was clear that she was hoping I would catch on to how pissed she was and would indulge her little temper tantrum. Much as it was tempting to just ignore it, I didn't like the feeling of the atmosphere between us.

14

"Go home," she replied curtly.

"And then?"

"Stay there."

I raised my eyebrows at her. I had seen her pissed before, but it had never been this bad. It had never seemed aimed directly at me before, and it was enough to throw me entirely off my normal game. I liked being with her, even when we weren't talking, but there was that friendly sort of quiet and then there was that heavy, weighted silence that seemed to come about every time she locked her eyes to the window again and pretended that I wasn't in the room.

"Planning the baby shower?" I pressed. I was already getting irritated with the way she was acting, but she hadn't liked it when I had snapped at her before. I wasn't going to make the same mistake again. By the time we got off this flight, I knew she was going to be back on my side again. I just needed to find the right way to approach it, to make it feel like she had come to the decision herself, not been guided in that direction by me.

"I don't know," she shot back. "Probably not."

"You need any help with that, you know where I am," I replied.

She snorted with amusement.

"What?" I demanded, feeling a little defensive.

She eyed me for a moment. "Sorry, but you don't strike me as the baby-shower type," she pointed out, eyeing me for a moment.

What the hell did she mean by that? Baby-shower type? Was I meant to walk around with color swatches for frosting at all times or something?

"Try me," I replied.

She shook her head. "I'd rather not."

With that, she'd fallen silent again for most of the rest of the flight, and I figured I was done trying to coax a response out of her. She needed some time to sit with her thoughts, and that was fine. Maybe we could get a drink when we got back, once I had dealt with the shit that my father had put out there, and then we'd be laughing about this by the end of the evening. That was what I wanted. I wanted it more than anything.

But when we got home, she'd grabbed her bags, climbed into a cab, and pulled away from me for good, making it about as clear as she could that she didn't want to spend another minute with me. Shit, I would have been lying if I said it didn't sting a little, but maybe that was what she needed. Maybe that was what I deserved for being so short with her that morning.

I expected her to text me when she got home, but she didn't even bother with anything like that. Okay, shit, I knew now that I had really done something wrong. Normally, she would throw something in my direction to let me know that she had gotten home safely. But now it seemed as though she was making a point to put distance between us. And that was starting to get seriously under my fucking skin.

Returning to my place, I tried not to think about her, but that was hard when it felt like everything I did would have been better if she'd been there to share it with me. Shit, when did I get so damn clingy? I wasn't sure that I liked this version of me, but I was going to have to get used to him since he seemed to be here to stay.

But shit, there was something about standing alone in the cold and the quiet of this apartment that made me feel as though I needed to make some noise. Anything just to cover up the silence that seemed to be inching into every part of my body. How was it that she could have this sort of power over me? It just didn't make any sense.

At the same time, it was the only thing that did make any sense. Because those few days we'd had together felt so perfect. Once we had gotten over the part where we weren't quite sure what we wanted from one another. But once that was behind us, once we had just given in and rolled into bed together, we started having a good time once more.

I had known it was going to go that way from the start. I might not have been willing to admit it, even to myself, but when I had booked that trip, I had booked it with getting with her in the back of my mind.

There was no other reason to have booked the single bungalow for us. No other reason to have taken her so far from home just to pay her back on a bet. The bet was a golf trip, but I'd made sure she had a spot at the most expensive resort in the country. That was something that friends didn't do for other friends, and I had known that somewhere at the back of my mind, even before we had stepped on that jet together.

But now it was over. The trip had ended badly and I was sure that I'd been the one to fuck it up. She had spoken to me like I was some sort of asshole when we were on the plane heading back home. I still wasn't quite sure what had brought that on.

Well, okay, maybe I hadn't been all sunshine and lollipops since I had gotten the call from back home, but that didn't mean she had to launch herself at me like I'd killed her puppy or something.

Shit, maybe I should have been a little nicer. Sometimes, I forgot what was required to handle people in my personal life. It had been so long since I'd had anyone by my side like her. I had just clicked out of the habit of how to talk to people properly in a way that didn't just reduce them from someone important to me to someone who just happened to be in the line of fire when something went wrong. Maybe that was why she had been so mad at me.

Maybe I needed to get my head out of my ass and focus on what really mattered here. Because there was a reason I had come back to the city, and it wasn't so I could sit around brooding about what had happened with Lilah. That was for damn sure. I had bigger things to deal with right now—like the fact that my father had decided to take advantage of my being out of town to get what he wanted from me.

I still couldn't believe he had really ignored what I had asked of him like that. Shit, I'd known he was an asshole for a while, but this was a whole new level of asshole, even for him, and I was pissed beyond belief that he would dare to use this shit against me in this way. I had a successful life of my own outside of him, and he hated that I had managed to establish myself in the world of business when he couldn't. He had proved over and over that he had no damn idea what he was doing with his life.

He had basically claimed that I was working with him on this specific deal, which had led to a couple clients who had worked with me before agreeing to invest with him. They thought I was behind it all. In short, this was bad news for me, and I had to make sure that I could find some way to put as much distance between me and him before he damaged my business reputation along with his own.

I went to bed that night with some video playing on my phone, not wanting to go to sleep all by myself without anything there to keep me company. By the time I woke up the next morning, I felt a little more determined.

Of course, I could handle this. I didn't care what my father threw in my direction. I could handle it. And okay, so Lilah had talked a big game about being done with me completely when we had been on that plane, but there was no way she actually meant it.

She needed this job, and she would be waiting there by the time that I got in, a sheepish look on her face and maybe even an apology. We could move past it and pretend it never happened if that was what she wanted.

I headed to the gym before I went to work, I dressed in my best suit, and I told myself that I was going to get everything under control. So my father thought he could prop up his failing business by risking my reputation, did he? I wasn't going to let him anywhere close.

There were a lot of guys out there who looked up to their fathers as examples of how to move through the world, but honestly, I was fairly sure that my dad was basically a cautionary tale for me and nothing more. I didn't want a damn thing to do with him, and I sure as hell didn't intend to follow in his footsteps.

He had made such a shit-stain mess of his business that he spent most of his middle age trying to piece together some sort of respectable business reputation from the scraps that he could steal by association with my name.

As I strode into the office, I fully expected to see Lilah sitting at the desk that sat outside my room. She was such a fixture there now that I could almost imagine what it would be like when I saw her there again—the little smile she would give me, the way she would announce the news for the day, the meetings that I had ahead of me, everything that I had to handle. She would often come in with some sort of breakfast to boot because I had a habit of forgetting that I had to eat or I would get pissy around lunchtime because I had failed to chow down on anything that morning.

I had missed her the night before. Lying in bed without her had been strange, especially after we had spent so much time together at the resort. I knew that it was a big change for us, coming back to the city and back to the real world where we would be expected to slip back into our real lives, but I was sure that we could make it work.

It was going to be tough for a while, and I certainly had an apology ready so I could tell her that I understood the way I'd acted just wasn't okay. I would reassure her that we would work this out. We had to. Because if we didn't work this out, I had no idea how I was meant to stick around this office without getting stuck on her all over again.

It was strange to think that there had been a point in time when I had been so against the idea of even having her in this place with me. My mom had gone undercover to sneak her into the office as my new personal assistant, convinced that she would make my life better. As it turned out, she actually had made my life better, just not in the way I had been expecting. Not in the way that even the most forward-thinking person in the world could have expected.

But when I rounded the corner, I found myself looking at an empty seat in front of me. My heart sank. Okay, she might be late for some reason. Even though she almost always got to the office before I did.

As I got a little closer, I saw that her desk had been cleared of nearly everything that would indicate she had ever been there at all. The couple of books she had stacked next to her keyboard, the note with the codes to everywhere scribbled on it in her handwriting. All of it was gone.

And sitting there in the middle of it all was a small envelope with my name on it. I picked it up, flipped it over in my hands, and looked down at the seal for a moment. I knew what was inside, and I didn't want to open it because opening it would have been accepting that this was real, and that was the last thing I wanted to acknowledge just then.

I strode into my office and slammed the door behind me. I knew that there was nobody around to hear it but me, but that didn't make it any less satisfying. Letting out a huge sigh, I sank into the chair behind my desk and planted the letter in front of me.

It didn't have an address on it or anything, so she must have come by to deliver this herself—at the same time she cleared out all her stuff, no doubt.

How early had she come in to make sure there was no chance of running into me? And why had she tried to avoid me so completely? Was the thought of seeing me again really that awful to her?

I had hoped the two of us had spent enough time together now that we didn't have those problems, but clearly, whatever she had seen from me on that trip had been enough to ensure she didn't want to see me again. At least not anytime soon.

"All right, let's see what you have to say for yourself," I muttered as I flipped the letter over in my hands and checked to see what I had waiting for me. Tearing the envelope open, I unfolded the paper that had been stuffed inside and skimmed over what I had in front of me.

It was written formally—that was the first thing that jumped out at me—as though she wanted to make sure that not a hint of the actual emotion she felt toward me came through in the typed-out text. The only hint that she had been the one to write this at all was the scrawl of her signature at the bottom, confirming that this really was from her and that she really meant this. It was a letter of resignation, forfeiting her severance pay and making sure she didn't have to step one foot over the threshold of this place ever again if she didn't want to.

I crumpled the letter into a ball and tossed it at the trashcan. It missed because of course it did. That was just my luck. Nothing had gone right since I had gotten that call from my office telling me what the fuck my father was dragging me into, and it didn't look like I was going to get a break anytime soon.

Rubbing my hand over my face, I tried to calm myself down. I could handle this. I had handled worse, hadn't I?

The thought of doing all of this without Lilah at my side to help me through it seemed more than any man could possibly handle alone.

Chapter Three

Lilah

AS VIOLET CAME THROUGH the door and saw me flapping the tea towel at the smoke detector, she burst out laughing.

"All right, I suppose I deserve that," I said.

"Here, let me," she ordered, and she grabbed the towel so that she could take over fixing the mess that I had made of dinner.

I dived toward the oven and pulled out the pasta bake I had been trying to put together, which had turned into a lightly charred wreck since I had forgotten that it was even in there in the first place.

Not going into work, it seemed, didn't really suit me so well. I had woken up this morning to the normal alarm that I had forgotten to turn off. Usually, I would have been delighted to find that I had a little more time to sleep. But today, I wanted nothing more than to have to drag my ass out of bed and head toward the office for the day. At least it would have been something to do. I needed that right now.

I had dreamed about Damian the night before, exactly the actions of someone who was utterly over somebody else. I had tried to keep my mind distracted when I had been awake, but when I had been sleeping, my brain had drawn me back to him once more, whether I liked it or not. I honestly couldn't say for sure if I did one way or the other.

In my dream, we had been on the plane, flying back to the city, and I had been trying to ignore the conversation he kept passing my way. But I couldn't.

It seemed as though his voice had gotten louder and louder the more I tried to ignore it. As long as I kept pretending that it wasn't there, it was only going to get worse and worse. When I had woken up with a start, I reached over to the other side of the bed to feel him there. The pump of his heart beneath his skin was usually all it took to calm me down, but I was there alone, and I remembered all at once what had forced us apart in the first place.

Waking up without him had been awful. I hadn't realized how much I would miss it until it actually happened. There was something about the weight of not feeling him in bed next to me that was heavier and harder than anything I had been ready for.

I should have prepared myself for this, but it was hard when it felt like we had just been falling into that happy little routine that made everything easier to deal with. Okay, so it was hardly perfect, but I thought that we could work toward something that was.

There were going to be some growing pains—I knew that much—but when he was with me, it felt like he was far different than the man I had known before. I could convince myself that he was different at least.

Maybe that was just what I had been doing. Telling myself over and over again that he was different, that he could learn to be different, that the two of us being together was enough for him to start undoing the stress that had wracked every part of him until I had become a part of his life.

His mother had been right, even if he would never admit it. He had needed an assistant. Someone who was willing to come in and take some of the weight off his shoulders. But now that weight seemed to have piled on again, and I felt guilty for being the one to take a step back when he needed me most.

No, I wasn't going to let myself think that way. I had to protect myself and my own heart first. Nothing was going to change that. No matter how guilty I might have been, no matter how badly I was beating myself up for going on the trip in the first place, that wasn't my problem anymore. Sometimes, people let you down, and that was just the way it happened to be. I felt like I should have known that by now, given everything that I had gone through with my ex.

Violet had already left for work by the time I dragged my ass out of bed, and I decided that the best course of action was to start cleaning the apartment from top to bottom to keep myself busy. Well, and also to give Violet a reason to keep me around now that I wouldn't be able to pay rent again. She had already put up with so much from me, and I couldn't believe I was on the brink of letting her down again.

I scrubbed the floors, cleaned the toilet, made the beds, even did a load of laundry and dried the clothes afterward so that they would be ready to wear by the time Violet came back. I convinced myself as I worked that this was something I could get used to. It wasn't ideal, but perhaps I could do the housewife thing. The house-roommate thing. Something like that.

Though I wasn't much of a cook, I was determined to have something on the table when Violet got back. I managed to find a recipe that promised foolproof pasta bakes. I figured if they were calling it that, I could pull it off.

But when Violet got back, the apartment was starting to fill with smoke, and the smoke alarm was screeching so loud that it felt like it was scolding me personally. She managed to coax it into silence once more, and I sighed and leaned on the counter.

"I'm sorry," I said. "I wanted to have dinner for you by the time you got back."

"Nothing wrong with ordering pizza," she replied as she grabbed the menus from the drawer next to the stove. "You want your usual?"

"Yeah, that would be great," I said, a little sheepish. I didn't want her to think I was just going to mooch off her from here on out while I didn't have a job. I counted out the change in my purse to make sure that I could cover my half of the order. When I handed it to her, Violet looked up at me, eyebrow cocked.

"What's this for?"

"The pizza," I said. "I don't want you to have to pay for my half. Go on. Take it."

"Hey, you deep cleaned this entire place today," she said. "I'm sure I can afford it."

"I'm sorry." I sighed, sinking into the couch across from her and dropping the coins and bills on the table. "I'm sorry for all of this."

"What do you mean?"

"I mean, I'm going to start looking for somewhere else to live," I said. "I can't keep expecting you to cover for me just because I don't have a job again."

"You don't have a job, so you're going to look for somewhere you won't be able to cover your rent?" She shook her head. "That sounds really logical."

"I can't keep staying here, though," I said. "It's not fair. You've already given me so much, and I don't have much built up in the way of savings. I'm not going to be able to cover my rent for much longer."

"You know that you can stay here as long as you need to," she told me gently.

The softness in her voice caught me off guard, and I felt a lump in my throat. I swallowed it down right away.

She nodded. "We just need to get you back out there and looking for a new job, don't we? We can figure this out. We just need to apply a little ingenuity to it."

Before she could say anything else, the doorbell buzzed, and I jumped to my feet to grab us our pizza.

"You find us something trashy to watch," I ordered her. "Come on. I could use some good old-fashioned nonsense."

Sure enough, she was able to dig up an old episode of *Say Yes to the Dress* that was being re-broadcast as part of a marathon, and the two of us got lost in keeping up with the ridiculous drama that unfolded as the mother-in-law-to-be snottily informed her new family member just what she thought of her dress.

We laughed along at the silliness, and I was thankful I had such a wonderful friend who was always willing to help me.

Sometimes, I felt like I didn't deserve someone like her, like I didn't deserve a friend who was there to have my back when I needed her the most, but maybe I had done something to earn keeping her around.

When we had finished our pizza, I insisted on clearing up, and when I came back to join Violet, she had poured us both a glass of wine and had her laptop propped up on her lap.

"What are you looking at?" I asked.

She turned it around to show me. It was a blank resume page, one that looked as though it was just waiting to be filled out.

"I think we should get you moving on a new resume," she said. "Don't you? If you're going to stop mooching off me sooner rather than later and all."

"Hey, don't be subtle about what you want," I joked as I sat down next to her and looked at the screen. "I already have one, though. Couldn't I just use that?"

"I think we need to start from scratch," she replied. "We need to look at everything you've done properly. And everything that you learned at the office. Maybe you could even re-apply there? For the job you went for in the first place?"

"I don't think they'd still have the position open," I said. "And besides, I really don't want to be around him, not if I can help it. I think it's best for both of us if I put as much space between us as possible."

"Point taken," she said, and she handed the laptop over to me. "Okay, so come on. What extra-curriculars did you do in high school?"

Soon enough, we had launched ourselves down the long and involved path of putting together a new resume for me from scratch. It was actually kind of fun, doing it with her around, and I found myself getting into it. Violet was much more willing to talk up my good traits than I was, and she was always quick to snatch the computer away from me and fill in the details that I felt a little too polite to put in myself.

"What are you going to say about why you left the last job?" she asked me as we rounded the corner on our second glass of wine and had nearly finished the resume.

"I don't know," I said. "I don't want to give too much away. I don't want them thinking that they should get in touch and follow up or anything."

"Hmm, yeah," she said. "What if you put *personal reasons*? If you say that, they're not going to delve any deeper. And if they do, you'll at least have had the time to come up with something more believable."

"Yeah, I guess so," I said.

She added it to the bottom of the resume. I stared at the words as they appeared on the screen in front of me. Personal reasons. That just sounded so distant somehow. It couldn't come close to telling the truth of everything that had happened between us. It was more than personal. It was something deeper, more confusing than that. *Personal reasons* didn't sum it up very well at all.

But what else could I say? That I had fallen for my boss, at least for some part of him that I wasn't even sure had ever actually existed? That he had shown the truth of who he really was to me, and I had stormed out like I had never wanted to know him in the first place? It all sounded crazy.

Violet was right. I was going to need to come up with something a little less scandalous if I was going to explain this away at some job interview somewhere down the line.

"Well, I think that's about as good as we're going to get tonight," Violet said to me as she saved the file and downloaded it just to make sure I had everything I needed.

"Thanks so much for this, Vi," I told her. "I don't know what I did to deserve a friend like you."

"You're too sweet," she replied. "And you've had far too much wine for me to take that seriously."

"Okay, I'll say it again when I'm sober then," I called after her as she got to her feet to go pour herself another glass.

I needed to keep myself busy for the rest of the night. The less time I spent thinking about Damian, about the job I had just left, and about everything that had happened to my life in the time since I had last been in this apartment, the better.

Besides, I had bigger things to think about now. After all, my mom had asked me to make sure I put together one hell of a baby shower for my sister, and I figured that I should get moving on that.

Maybe I would find out I had a secret passion and skill for putting together baby showers or something. That this had been my calling all along, and all I needed to do was embrace it and I would finally be able to do everything I needed to with my life.

Yes, I liked that idea. I liked it a lot. Or maybe I'd just had too many glasses of wine and needed to calm down before my imagination got the better of me.

"You want to help me do some baby-shower planning?" I asked Violet as she came back over to join me.

She clapped her hands together, a giant smile spreading across her face. "You better believe I do! Where do we start? Okay, so I actually did a little research into the best places in the city for baby showers, and I think I've come up with a few good places to start."

"Hit me," I replied. "You know that I don't have a clue how any of this works."

With that, the two of us lost ourselves to the task ahead of us.

And for just a little while, I was able to put Damian out of my head.

Chapter Four

Damian

I CHECKED MY PHONE for the third time that day to see if Lilah had bothered to get back to me yet, but there was nothing waiting for me.

This wasn't something I was used to. People didn't usually ignore my calls, and there was something about being brushed off in this way that made the hair on the back of my neck stand on end.

All I wanted to do was talk to her. That was it. That was all. It might have looked bad to her, but I wasn't asking for her attention, her affection, her adoration, or anything like that. I just wanted to speak to her so we could clear the air and I could convince her to come back to work and stop making a fool of herself over something that she didn't need to.

Emotion wasn't something I had ever been good at. My parents used to tease me about it when I had been younger, when I had been this deadly serious kid who was growing up with a frown on his face. My mom used to tell me that they had tried everything to get me to lighten up, but I had never been the kid who wanted to play with his friends—not when I could have been spending time working on the homework I had to take care of anyway.

I supposed that had spread into my adulthood, too. When it came to having people around me who I trusted, people who were there just for fun, I wasn't particularly good at that side of things.

I sometimes wished I could have been the guy who was cooler, who was free and easy and could come at any situation and make everyone feel at home, but that had never been who I was. I was pretty sure it was too late for me to learn now, no matter how much I might have liked to shift things. At a certain point, the way you were was just the way you were always going to be.

Hell, I hadn't even been able to let Lilah into my life as anything other than my assistant, not at first. It was sort of crazy now that I thought of it. I could still remember the first time we had run into each other, when she had stood up and chewed me out right there in front of my mother, making sure that I knew just where she stood and that she wasn't going to take a word of my nonsense from me.

Maybe that had been the moment I started to fall for her, even though I had tried to pretend otherwise. When she had made me feel that spark of emotion, something which I usually fought so hard to keep to myself.

Shit. I was still thinking about her like that. As someone I had fallen for. I couldn't let myself do that any longer. Not when she wouldn't even talk to me.

I had never been the guy who spent his time running around after someone that didn't want him. Normally, I knew just when to take off the pressure to keep myself from looking like a total idiot, but these days, it felt like she had tossed the game pieces off the board, and now I was scrambling to pick them all up again. The rules were broken, and I didn't know where to even start on playing the game anymore.

I hadn't heard a word from her since she had stormed away from me at the airport and caught a cab back to her place, and it was starting to drive me nuts. People didn't ignore me. Nobody ignored me. Nobody was stupid enough to do that. A call from me was something people wanted to bend over backward to hear about, even if it meant dropping everything they were already doing just to speak to me about whatever it was that I needed to talk about.

There was only one person in this entire city that I actually wanted to talk to right now, and she was making it pretty fucking clear that she didn't want anything to do with me. I felt like I was losing my mind.

Where the hell did she get off treating me like this? She couldn't just duck my calls and expect me to drop everything. I didn't want to make a big deal out of this. I was just trying to do the right thing by clearing the air, but she wasn't even going to give me the chance to do it? It was a cruel move, and I didn't like that she had me on the hook and falling for it.

I could have turned up at her house, of course, but I figured it would be in direct conflict with the vibe I was trying to throw out right now. I didn't want her to think I was desperate, or that I couldn't stop thinking about her, or that I would act out in some stupid way just to get her back. I was cool, I was calm, I was collected, and I just wanted to know one way or the other what I had done to scare her off so badly that she had even quit her job on top of everything else.

She had needed that position. I knew that. She had made it pretty clear to me that she was trying to get herself on her own two feet to make sure she never had to worry about that again, but whatever had happened between us had been enough to scare her all the way away from me, and now, she was back out on the job market once more. That was what bothered me more than anything.

I had really thought she was just saying all that stuff when she'd told me she was done with me. So to come into work and find out she had meant every word had been enough to make me feel like the ground was sliding out from under me, threatening to toss me off the edge if I wasn't careful.

I fucking hated this. I couldn't get in touch with her, and my father had been making a point to avoid all of my calls as well. The only two people in the city I actually needed to talk to were acting like I didn't exist, and it felt like I was starting to lose my mind thanks to the two of them combined.

This was what I got for taking my hands off the wheel, if only for a moment or two. I thought that taking that trip with her would just be a chance to blow off some steam, but all it had done was land me in more trouble than I knew what to do with. It wasn't right, but I knew it was all my fault, and nothing was going to change that.

I would never make this mistake again. I would never let myself believe that I could just unlatch from the reality of what my life needed from me and forget that I had any responsibilities at all. The world had come by to give me a pretty harsh reminder that I was never going to get away with that, and this time, I was going to listen to it and not make the same mistake again.

I tried to keep myself busy with work, but I couldn't stop thinking about Lilah and what she might have been doing. Was she thinking about me? I had to know.

My brain seemed to itch whenever I thought of her. The pain of not being able to reach out and just ask was driving me mad. Maybe I should just turn up at her place and find out what was going on. Wasn't that what she had shown me in some of those movies? Taking the initiative, going out and seeking the woman you wanted. Though I doubted that those ideas would play quite as well in real life.

When I returned from my meeting with legal, I headed back upstairs to the office to grab some files I would need to handle my next client. I found my mother there, leaning on the desk that had belonged to Lilah and looking at me with an expectant expression on her face.

"What are you doing here?" I asked her, already feeling a little impatient that she had just rolled up and decided to make a nuisance of herself.

"Oh, that's a nice way to greet your mother," she replied, and she nodded to the desk she was leaning on. "Where did she go by the way? None of her stuff is here. What happened?"

Shit. I knew this conversation was going to have to happen at one time or another, but I had hoped I might have a little more time to come up with something that would actually satisfy her curiosity. I shook my head and shrugged.

"We decided that she wasn't a good fit here," I replied, keeping my voice as neutral as possible. I had no idea if Mom knew about the trip I had taken out of town, and I prayed that she didn't. That would only lead to more questions, questions I didn't have any real answers to.

She would sniff them out of me—I was sure of it—and frankly, the last thing I needed right now was her poking around inside my head when I wanted nothing more than to just be left alone.

"That doesn't make any sense," she replied, blunt as ever. "I saw the way the two of you worked together. You were really good together. What did you do to make a mess of it?"

"I didn't do anything," I said at once, far more defensive than I needed to be. "Why would you just assume that I was the one to mess it up?"

"Because I know she needed the job, and I don't think she was the one who would have made a mess of it," she said. "Is she gone then? Does she have to do her two weeks first?"

"No, she's gone," I replied. "We decided it was what was best for the both of us."

"Oh, really?" Mom replied, and she eyed me for a moment.

I looked back at her, trying to keep my face as calm as possible, and hoped that she didn't exercise some of her parent powers to see into my head and figure out what was going on in there.

"Really," I replied. "Why are you so concerned about her anyway? I thought you just wanted to get me an assistant."

"Yes, well, she seems like a nice girl, and I'm sure that she wouldn't have left of her own accord," she said. "She was good for you, wasn't she? She made your life easier?"

"That's not really important," I shot back, my voice taut and pointed. I didn't want to have this conversation with her. I didn't want to have this conversation with anyone.

Being in the office without Lilah to keep me company was hard enough without people turning up to ask questions about where she might have gone to.

"I should check in with her," she muttered.

I instantly shook my head. "No, you should just leave her be."

I could tell I had sparked some curiosity in her head. She cocked it to the side and looked up at me, narrowing her eyes as though trying to figure out what was going on in my mind.

"What happened, son?" she asked.

I knew it was my last chance to come clean to her about everything that had gone down between us. But if she found out, she might want to push for me to pick up where we had left off, and I was far too stubborn to do something like that. Lilah had made it pretty clear that she wanted to move on, and I wasn't going to put any pressure on her to come back and pick up where she had left off.

"Nothing happened," I told her. "She wasn't a good fit here. That was it. Sometimes, these things don't work out. Especially when you're applying for a job that you didn't even know existed until you walked into the office."

"Point taken," Mom said. Her voice was a little strained, like there was more she wanted to say but she had no clue how to come out and say it to me.

I stared back at her, daring her to call me on it, daring her to tell me that I had done something wrong and that I needed to make amends.

"But if there was something that happened," she said, speaking slowly, carefully, as though she was worried that she might scare me off if she went too fast. "Then you know I would find out about it eventually. I am your mother, after all. You know you can't keep anything from me, don't you?"

"Oh, I know," I replied grimly. I just had to hope Lilah could keep her mouth shut and not spill anything to anyone who might get it back to my dear mother, lest I suffer her wrath for fucking up what she had so carefully put in place for me.

"Well, I'm glad to hear it," she said. She gave me one last look, turned on her heel, and marched out of the office.

As soon as she was gone, I felt a weight lift from my shoulders. She wasn't going to let it go that easily, but at least for now, I had managed to deflect her curiosity.

The last thing I needed was my mother sticking her nose into my business.

Chapter Five

Lilah

"WELL, LILAH, I HAVE to say we're really impressed with everything that we're seeing here," Sally told me with a smile. She was the owner of the coffee shop where I had my third interview of the day.

"Thank you," I replied, and I tried my best to return her grin. I wasn't sure that it reached my eyes, but she was already looking back at the freshly printed page of my resume in front of her. I told myself things were going to be just fine.

One day had been enough to sit around and feel sorry for myself. The morning after our wine-and-pizza night, I had gotten out of bed and headed down to the streets to start handing out my resume and applying for new jobs.

I supposed that was something I had picked up from my family. Even though I tried to distance myself from them inside my own head every chance I got, for the time being, I was glad I could hear them in the back of my mind, telling me to get off my ass and do something. The last thing I wanted was to turn up for that baby shower—whenever the hell I planned the damn thing for—feeling sorry for myself. I had to put on my game face or else they would all see that I had managed to walk myself ass-backward into one hell of a mess.

So far, I had been avoiding Damian's calls as best I could, but every time they sprang up on my phone, I found myself wondering if I should just give in and answer him. What harm could it do? Just to hear his voice again. That was it. That was all.

But something told me I had to hold back. I couldn't just give him what he wanted, not after he had hurt me so badly. The part of me that wanted everyone to like me was already tempted to pick up the phone and just tell him that it was all forgotten and we could move on now, but there was some small, resilient part of me that told me I should stand my ground.

Maybe that was what they called growth. After the last breakup I'd had—not that I was even sure if I could call what I had with Damian a breakup—I had felt like the whole world had been ripped out from underneath me. Like I would never manage to get myself right again.

I could still remember the awful sick sensation that brought the knowledge that nothing would be the same again and that I would never be able to catch up with the way it had been before. I was sure I would never be able to put my life back together. Hell, I didn't even know what a life looked like without my ex.

But I had managed then, and I would manage now. We had only spent a few days together being an actual couple anyway. It would be easier to move on from that than it had been from my ex. I was sure of it.

At least, that was what I had to keep telling myself because I couldn't find any other good reason that all of this was happening—why the hurt was so bad. I missed him like hell. And on top of all that, I had to find a new job too.

A couple of them had been willing to meet with me later that week, which was how I found myself sitting opposite this smiling older woman who seemed eager to hire me as a waitress in her coffee shop.

I knew that I had to take whatever came my way, but in all honesty, I didn't really like the idea of working at a place like this. It paid fine, and it was close to the apartment, so I knew I couldn't really get any better than that, but it just felt like such a step down from working with Damian. I would have to be around people all day instead of just spending my eight-hour shifts handling one person and getting to laze around behind a desk as much as I wanted.

Here, I was going to have to be around people all day long, going to have to keep that smile on my face no matter what, and the thought of it was already starting to get under my skin and make me feel like I was getting hives. I knew I was overreacting, that I needed a job more than I needed time to myself to sit around at the apartment and feel even more useless than I had before, but still, I didn't know if I could do this.

I focused on the interview and kept the smile on my face, and by the time we were done, she was already on her feet and showing me how to work the coffee machine behind the counter. Just in case I started work there, of course. I tried to take in everything that she was saying to me, even though my head felt like it was stuffed with so much else I could hardly cram any more on top of it.

When we finished, she shook my hand and offered me a big friendly grin.

"Thanks so much for coming in today," she told me. "We really appreciate it. I'm extremely impressed with your application."

"That's great to hear," I replied, hoping that my enthusiasm was coming off as genuine.

She walked me to the door and waved me off, and I let out a breath the minute I stepped out onto the street outside. It was over. It was totally and utterly over. I could just go home, change into comfy clothes, and hope I had done enough to get back in the job market.

Violet had loaned me an outfit for the day, something that would give me a little pep in my step, and I knew she would want it cleaned and ready for her by the time she got back. She had a meeting at the end of the week that she needed to look sharp for, and I wasn't going to let her down. She had already done so much to support me, and the least I could do was make sure she had everything she needed to achieve success.

I was putting away the clothes and slipping into my comfy sweats when I got a text from the woman who owned the coffee shop. She was offering me the job.

I stared at the screen for a second, sure that I must have been misreading it somehow, but no, it was really her, and she really wanted me to have that position. I felt a wave of relief—I was going to be able to pay rent—and then a wave of dread when I realized I was actually going to have to do the job.

I texted back to say I would love to work with her before I could talk myself out of it. Then I called Violet to let her know how things had gone.

"Oh my goodness, that's fantastic!" she squealed down the line. "We should celebrate!"

I laughed. "I think I'm good on the celebrating for now, but how about we pencil it in for the weekend?"

"Sure, but I'm buying cake for when I get home," she said. "We need to make a big deal out of this! You know how long people spend looking for jobs, and you got another one in a week? That means you must have made a really good impression on her."

I could have sworn that Violet seemed more excited than I was, and I wondered if I was being ungrateful by not being so thrilled about the new job that I had just landed.

I ended the call with Vi, and I felt like a heavy weight had settled onto my shoulders. Not that I wasn't glad to have a new job, of course, but it would be a step down from what I had before. I probably wouldn't be able to find another job even close to as good as that one for a hell of a long time, if ever again.

Not to mention the fact that I was never going to have a boss like Damian again. It was for the best really, given the mess that getting involved with him had made of my life, but still, it had been nice to have someone around who seemed to like me for more than just the work I did. I missed him, and getting over that wasn't going to happen as long as I was sitting on my ass and just waiting for—

Suddenly, there was a knock at the door, and I jumped. Was Violet back already?

No, it couldn't be her. She wouldn't have knocked.

I went to the door and pulled it open. When I saw who was standing there on the other side waiting for me, my jaw dropped.

"Melanie?" I blurted out. "What are you doing here?"

"I hope I'm not intruding," she replied as she straightened her jacket and seemed to ignore my reaction totally. "I wanted to stop by after I found out that you and my son had stopped working together."

I opened my mouth to ask how she had found out, but I figured it was best just to play dumb with her. Where she was concerned, I'd gotten the feeling she could dig up anything in the world if she ever set her mind to it, especially when it came to her son, and I was just an extension of that.

"I wanted to know what it was that made you decide to leave," she said.

My mind flashed back to my resume. I still hadn't come up with anything better than that, so I just shrugged and repeated it once more.

"Personal reasons," I told her.

She grimaced, looking as though that was the last thing she wanted to hear. "I thought you would be such a good fit for the office," she replied with a sigh. "Are you sure there's nothing I can do to convince you to come back?"

"I've already found another job," I told her, and I felt a little hint of pride, knowing that I could say so and actually mean it.

Her eyes widened. "Already?"

I nodded. "Yes, already."

"I'm sure we would be able to see our way to bumping up your wages," she said.

I had to contain a little smirk of amusement. Damian had always told me his mom thought of herself as part of his work, even though she had no reason to. It was clear she was acting that out even now.

"It's not about the money," I told her. "I just have other things that need my attention right now."

She sighed again and glanced around, as though fearful we were being listened to. "I don't want to put too much pressure on you, but you have to understand how good you were for my son. He'd never admit it himself, but I think he needs the sort of help you gave to him. If you could see your way to coming back, I'm sure we could figure out a way to overcome any of the problems that you may have been having."

"Melanie, I really appreciate it, but I need to move on," I replied as gently as I could.

She was just trying to help her son, but I couldn't be around to cover for him any longer. He had to deal with his own shit. I had to get on with my life, and I had to start doing that now before I got caught up in the thought of what we could have had together—what we could have shared if things had just gone a little differently.

"Look, just give it a few days before you take the job at the new place," she said. "I can go down there and kick his ass. Till the end of the week, all right? That's all I'm asking for."

As the older woman stood in front of me, I knew there was no way to get rid of her unless I just caved and gave her a chance. She didn't strike me as the sort of woman who backed down from a challenge easily, and right then, she saw me as a challenge.

I shrugged and nodded. "Sure."

At worst, it would just let Damian know that I had moved on with my life—and that I was in demand with more people than just him. A little childish, sure, but I felt like I deserved the chance to boast around a little bit, given what had happened between us.

"Thank you," Melanie replied, and she rolled her shoulders back once more as though pleased with the way all this had gone. "Thanks for your time, Lilah. Have a good weekend."

"You too," I replied, and with that, I closed the door.

That had been more than a little surreal. I knew that this woman was just trying to help out, to make things better for her son in the only way she knew how. I hoped it would be enough to keep her at bay for the time being.

In the back of my mind, I wondered if perhaps she had a point. Maybe I should have given things another shot. Maybe she would be the woman to make that happen.

As I headed back into the apartment, the new coffee-shop job was the last thing on my mind, and for the first time that day, the smile on my face was genuine.

Chapter Six

Damian

"CAN YOU PLEASE TELL him to call me as soon as he gets this message?" I asked the guy on the other end of the line before letting out a long sigh and rubbing my hand over my face.

"Yes, of course. As soon as he's back in the office, we'll let him know."

"No, sooner than that," I told him. "You tell my father that if he doesn't get back to me in the next two days, I'll be coming down there myself, and he's not going to want to have to deal with me. You understand?"

"Yes, sir, Mr. Cross," the man muttered. He seemed irritated by the way I was talking to him. Well, he could be as annoyed as he wanted. It wasn't going to keep me from telling him off when he needed to hear it.

For fuck's sake, I damn well should have heard from my father by now. With every moment that passed, I felt myself getting closer and closer to just letting what had happened with him slip. I couldn't let that happen again.

"Thank you," I replied, and I hung up the phone before I could go off on the man for another second. He hadn't signed up for this. He had just taken a job at an office, and he'd had no reason to think that it would turn into such a mess for him.

Shit, me too for that matter. The last few days had been a nightmare, and it felt like it was only just getting started. I didn't understand how I could have made such a mess of all this. It seemed like everything had just gone peeling apart at the seams as soon as I headed away for that trip. I only had myself to blame for it.

I would have liked to think I had more control of it than that, but it seemed as if I needed to be here to keep an eye on everything personally or else it would all fall apart in my absence.

Well, to be fair, it wouldn't have gone wrong if it hadn't been for my father sticking his nose where it didn't belong and making a mess of what I had worked so hard to build for myself. The more time that passed, the more time he spent avoiding my calls and the angrier and angrier I became. He knew he couldn't avoid me forever, but he was making a damn good attempt to do just that, the bastard.

This had been my father's MO the entire time I had been an adult, so I didn't know why it was coming as such a surprise to me now. Sometimes, it took me a second to remember that he was actually my dad and I was his son. Usually, the roles felt like they were so inverted that it was way too easy to forget that and just start taking care of him—because it seemed like what he needed.

Actually, the whole thing reminded me of his first wedding—well, the first one after he and my mom had split up for good. At that point, I had been about twenty, and the woman he was marrying had been maybe five years older than me.

That had been enough to get me feeling like there was already something seriously off with the way he was going about things, but I had put that to the back of my mind, convincing myself that this was just the way he was. This was just the way fathers were, and I needed to go along with what was happening because I had no right to argue against the way he chose to do things.

"You need to make sure that your mother doesn't come, son," he'd told me, speaking urgently on a call the day before I had planned to fly out to the resort where the two of them were getting married.

I had furrowed my brow, confused. "You know that she doesn't want to come out there and watch you get married, right?"

"I know what she's like," he said. "She's vindictive. I could see her turning up just to cause trouble."

"Pretty sure she couldn't care less, Dad," I replied.

"But you promise you'll do it, won't you?" he asked.

I let out a sigh. It wasn't really what I had expected, but hey, if it got him off my back.

"Yeah, I'll do it," I replied.

He'd hung up the phone without another word, clearly having gotten everything he wanted from me.

At the time, I should have seen it for what it was—him foisting all this responsibility on me when I was nothing more than a kid trying to help out. But that was always how he had been. Making his shit my problem. Making sure I felt totally and utterly responsible for the way his life went.

As soon as I was old enough to hold my own head up, it felt like he had been shifting blame for everything closer and closer to my door. This was no different. Except at least the wives had gotten a little older right along with him. That was a relief.

It seemed like my involvement in his drama was worse than I ever could have thought possible. He had leveraged my arrival at that dinner in order to prove that I was on board with what he was doing at his business, and everyone seemed to have believed him.

That was what I got for daring to be younger than him, for daring to be his son. Everyone just acted like he must have known best, even though every single thing about the way he had run his business so far proved the opposite.

He had basically put me on the line as collateral for the new deal he was trying to strike with some business from Yemen. They had worked with a company I had worked with a few years before, and that was what had gotten them in touch with my father in the first place.

He was using my good name to prove that he was worth the risk, and I needed to pull myself out of this mess before something terrible happened. I wasn't going down with him. He had made enough of a mess of his career already, and it wasn't my job to help him fix it. Not a chance in hell.

On top of that, all this time I had been trying to figure out just who was behind the disappearance of the prep work done prior to that first business trip that Lilah and I had taken. I still hadn't been able to figure that one out, but I needed to find out who it was before something worse happened. If there was someone here who was working against my best interests, I damn sure needed to figure out who it was and what they were up to.

By the time I headed home that day, I felt like I had just stepped out after six rounds in the ring. Like someone had beaten the shit out of me. I knew I was being dramatic, but I couldn't help it. Had I really done this every day before Lilah turned up? It seemed impossible to maintain, and it had only been a few days since she had moved on.

I had coped with the workload before she arrived, and I knew I would find a way to cope again. It was going to be a struggle, and I was going to have to get used to functioning in this world without her, but I would find a way to do it.

I got home and took a long shower, then ordered myself some food before I sat down in front of the TV to find something mindless to watch. My mind flicked back to that night of the storm when the two of us had snuggled up on the couch and watched movies together, getting more and more comfortable until there was nothing keeping us apart at all. Until we just moved against each other like it was natural and kissed and touched and—

I realized I was just staring at my own reflection in the TV, trying to make sense of the rush of memories that coursed through my mind. I missed her. Fuck, I missed her so much, and I felt like it was my fault that things between us had gone so wrong. I knew I was going to need to work double-time to find some way to make them right again—if I had any chance at all of doing so.

No, I wasn't going to let that get stuck in my head again. I had bigger and better things to think about. So some girl I had hooked up with a few times had decided to call things off? So what? My life didn't come grinding to a halt because of someone else. It never had and it never would. I wasn't going to make that mistake now.

Besides, it probably wasn't even Lilah I was actually missing. It was probably just having someone around the office who could make things run a little smoother. That was all I needed really. I just needed to get an assistant again. Then all of this would go away. This emptiness. This quiet inside my head that sometimes felt as though it was utterly deafening.

I could accept that my mom had been right about that. I needed someone around who made my life easier. No way was I going to admit that she had been right about Lilah, though. Hell, I didn't want her to know there was no good reason for it not working out as I had said, and if she caught on to that, she would do something crazy, like try to pay her off to come back or something.

Maybe I could get my mother on board with finding me a new assistant, since she seemed to have a good idea of what worked for me. Not that I would tell her that, of course. I didn't want her getting too used to the thought that she actually knew what was best for me, even though I got the feeling that she already believed it in every way that mattered. No, I could just pass it off to her to avoid taking on even more stress.

Who could replace Lilah? Well, there had to be a hell of a lot of people out there who could do the job she did. After all, she had never even done work like that before. She had walked in with no experience and she had pulled it off. So it couldn't be that hard.

I needed someone who was smart. Sharp. Someone who could handle everything the job threw at them without getting distracted or thrown off their game. Someone who was able to call me on my shit—yeah, Mom had told me that was the main reason for hiring Lilah in the first place, and it was clear she had been right about that.

But it had to be someone that I wasn't going to fall for. I didn't need that in my life again. Maybe I'd be best hiring a dude.

They could be territorial, and not many of them took direction from other guys well, but at least I would be guaranteed I wouldn't actually become attracted to them. Yeah, I should make sure I hired a man this time. It was the only way to be sure.

And maybe my father would find it a little harder to ignore the calls if I had some tough guy on the other end of the line, making sure that everything was taken care of.

My phone sprang to life beside me, and I answered it at once. My first thought was that it might be my father, but at the back of my mind, I wished that I would hear Lilah's voice coming down the line to tell me she was sorry. That she had been thinking about me. That she missed me and she wanted to see me again, and to forget everything she had said to me because she had been wrong and she had wanted me all this time.

"Hello, sir. This is your delivery driver. I'm outside the building but I can't figure out how to get in."

"I'll be there in a second." I sighed, hung up the phone, and went downstairs to let him into the building.

It hadn't been who I was hoping for, but that didn't mean anything. If there was anything to take from this, it was that I needed to find someone to replace Lilah as soon as I could so she didn't get too stuck inside my head. So I could move on and let go and forget about everything we had done together.

When someone replaced her, this would all stop. I was just caught up on what I wanted from her, even though I knew I couldn't get it again. I had made this mess for myself, and I sure as hell was going to find a way to put it right now that I was deep in the midst of it.

Was this perfect? No, but that didn't mean I couldn't fix it with a little determination and some quick thinking. And maybe by admitting that my mother had been right. Well, about some of it at least.

I greeted the guy at the door and grabbed my food from him, giving him a generous tip for his trouble. As I turned to head back up to the apartment with the steaming package in my arms, my mind started to tick.

There was a whole lot that I needed to take care of, but sometimes, I worked best under pressure.

And I just had to pray that now was one of those times.

Chapter Seven

Lilah

I SAT IN THE COFFEE shop, looking around, not sure what I was waiting for. That was when I saw him.

I had no idea what Damian was doing there, but it didn't matter. When our eyes met, everything else fell away.

How was it that even though we had spent all this time apart, seeing him still felt like a promise I wanted to follow through on?

I didn't know how he had found me, but I didn't care either. I got to my feet, my eyes burning into his, and he moved toward me and pulled me into his arms.

It was the kind of kiss that would get me fired from my new job at the coffee shop, but I found it difficult to give a damn. He kissed me hard and deep, his hands roaming over my back and my ass, pushing up the skirt I'd forgotten I put on that morning. I could feel the eyes of the patrons around us, but I didn't care. Shit, why would I? He was there with me, and that was all that mattered.

He pushed me back against the table behind me, a couple of chairs tipping over with a loud crash as I hooked my legs around him. I didn't even know how we were staying balanced, but I didn't care. All that mattered was the kiss, a kiss that felt like it could go on for a lifetime or more and would never get old.

His hands were underneath my skirt, his fingers pressing against my panties, his breath hot on my neck. He moaned against my ear, and suddenly, it was like everyone else who had been in that room before vanished. It was just us in the middle of nowhere, nothing to stop us or hold us back because we finally had each other.

He ripped my panties off and tossed them to the floor, and I arched my back from the table and pushed myself against him.

Yes, yes, *yes*. I needed this. I didn't even know how I had been able to hold back from it for so long. It didn't make sense to me. None of this did.

Had something happened between us to pull us apart? I couldn't remember, but if it had, I was sure it couldn't have actually mattered. Not really. Not when all that mattered was the way he pushed his fingers inside of me, fucking me with his hand roughly as he looked deep into my eyes.

Damn, those eyes of his. They drove me crazier than anything else. The way he looked at me like he couldn't get enough of me. Like all he wanted in the world was to make me come and there was nothing he wouldn't have done to achieve that aim.

He drew his fingers from between my thighs and pressed them to my lips, parting my mouth easily. I swirled my tongue around them, tasting him, tasting myself, tasting all of it.

"Fuck me," I gasped.

He didn't need to be told twice. A moment later, he had spread my legs wide, unzipped his pants, and slowly, slowly, slowly pushed himself inside of me. We should have been using a condom, but in that moment, I didn't give a damn. I wanted him. I wanted to feel him.

I let out a moan that seemed to travel right up from my guts to come out of my mouth, the pleasure of it more than I could take. The fullness—that was the best part. The way he made me feel as though I had been made to take him, but only just.

I had to bite my lip to keep from crying out, my pussy spreading to fit all of him inside me. He was so thick, so long, so perfect, and he kissed me as he drew himself into me once more, softening the edge of how far I was stretched with everything that his kiss gave to me.

I wound my arms around him, letting my hands slide down to his ass and pushing him deep inside of me.

How could I have let the time pass between this and the last moment we had been together? I couldn't remember what had kept us apart, not really, but I knew it didn't matter anymore. As long as the two of us were together, nothing mattered.

I just needed him so deeply and so truly that I couldn't think of anything else in the world that mattered to me right then. I could still taste my musk on my lips, could still feel the pressure of his fingers against me.

He was thrusting so hard that everything on the table was clattering with each movement. He was filling me over and over again, driving so deep it was making my whole body tremble. This was how much he had wanted me. This was how he had needed me. This was how we had craved each other, with such a burning hunger that nothing else even came close to mattering.

I moved my hand between my legs and stroked my clit, matching his pace. The decadence of the sensation was more than I could handle. It was like that first time we had been together, when being with him had been less of a pleasure and more a need, a burning desire that arched from deep inside of me, taking control of everything else. My mind was fading, my body hungering, and everything was slowing down so that I could be in this moment—right here, right now.

"Oh," I groaned against his neck, feeling the pulse of his heart against my mouth as I kissed him. I could smell his aftershave, the scent of it so familiar that it was almost like I could get lost in it. He drove me crazy—like my mind was giving in when we were together.

"Are you close?" His voice sounded less like it came from another person and more like it had emanated from deep inside of me.

I nodded. I could feel the lines between his body and mine starting to blur, just the way I liked it, just the way it had been when we had been wrapped up in each other in the midst of that thunderstorm, with the lights out and just the two of us together in the dark.

"I'm close," I whispered in return.

"Show me," he replied.

I pushed back against him, needy, hungry, showing him in every way that I wanted him. I had never wanted anyone the way I wanted him in that moment. I had fucked before, plenty of times, but it never felt like it did when I was with him. He pushed me to an edge I didn't even know existed. Something that felt dangerous and desperate, like I was hanging on by my fingertips.

"Yes," I murmured as I felt the pleasure course through me. "Yes."

"I want to feel you come, Lilah," he told me, his voice commanding, leaving no room for argument.

I pulled my knees back so that he could get even deeper inside of me, my fingers moving frantically against my clit, the pleasure burning up, growing, swelling till I could hardly take it anymore. And then—

"Lilah?"

A familiar voice snapped me back to reality, and I came flying out of my dream to be dumped, rather rudely, right back into my bed once more.

My hand was between my legs, and my covers were all a mess, but there was no denying the fact that my little fantasy had been nothing more than that—a fantasy.

"What?" I called back to Violet, who was standing on the other side of the door.

I wasn't sure that I wanted to look her in the eye anytime soon. I didn't know if she would be able to peer into my eyes and tell just what I had been up to. Living together had made me closer to her than almost anyone before, and it was strange how well she understood me.

"Are you all right? You were making some weird noises. I just wanted to see that you were okay."

"Oh—uh, yeah, I'm fine," I replied.

She sounded exhausted, and I wondered just how loud I'd been to wake her up in the middle of the night. I felt awful about it. I knew she needed her rest, and here I was, having a rampant dream encounter with a man who was meant to be out of my life for good. No wonder she sounded irritated.

"Good," she replied, and with that, I heard her feet padding down the corridor and back to her room again.

I slumped back on the pillow again and stared at the ceiling, suddenly wide awake and glad I didn't have to worry about going into work tomorrow.

If I'd had to look him in the eye after that, I was sure he would have been able to tell. Maybe he'd been having the same dreams about me.

Perhaps he had woken up in the same mood in the middle of the night, somewhere far across the city in a fancy apartment that was way nicer than mine. Did he reach for the empty part of the bed the same way I did? Did he wonder if I was thinking of him too?

I wished I could push my hand out through the night and find out.

What the hell was that? Why had my brain tossed that at me when I felt like I was finally moving on from him? Okay, so I had allowed Melanie to talk to him for me, but that was it. I wasn't following up on anything else with him. Not a chance in hell. No way, no how. I had better things to do than think about him, and yet my brain seemed determined to throw him back in my direction.

Maybe that was why. Maybe I was starting to get a little too far from him in my own head, and my mind didn't want me putting too much space between us, for fear that I would forget him entirely. Which was exactly what I was hoping would happen.

Or was I?

Maybe some part of me wasn't ready to let go yet. He was the first guy I had been with since I had split with my ex, after all, and that had to count for something.

And he had been romantic—at least a little anyway—when we had first gotten together and started with all of that. When we had been at the bungalow and he had whisked me off to that little picnic. When we had spent the day goofing off together and having a good time, it had all been enough for me to start to believe we could build something real.

But the more time that passed, the more it became clear that it had just been a mistake. A mistake that I wasn't going to repeat again. I had already let the coffee shop know that I would need a few days to get my shit together before I started work there, and they had been fine with that. Because I knew that Melanie wasn't going to be able to persuade her son to let me back into his life. Even if she did, that didn't mean I was going to hurry in and take him up on the offer.

I had to move on. I had a life to think about outside of him, and I wasn't going to let what had happened between us get stuck in my head and ruin what I was meant to be doing next. I had bigger and better things to focus on—my new job, the baby shower for my sister, starting over again.

Even if it meant going back to square one, at least I had learned something from what had happened with us. I would never let myself fall for someone I worked for again. Too complicated. A million times too complicated. I was smarter than that now, and nothing was going to make me repeat those same mistakes.

I turned over in bed, pulled the covers back over myself, and glared up into the darkness. Inside my head, I struck a bargain. If my sleeping brain could promise me that I was never going to have to deal with sex dreams like that again, I would do the absolute best I could to make sure my waking brain didn't spend too much time focusing on him either.

All the while, I knew I couldn't talk my brain out of being stuck on him. It didn't work like that. He had hooked into some part of me I knew I couldn't shake off so soon. I hadn't even known I had been lacking something until he had come along to show me just how much better my life was with someone in it. With someone who cared for me, someone who wanted me.

But that wasn't the version of him that existed all the time. That version chose to come and go as he pleased, and frankly, I wasn't much interested in trying to divine the movements of him one way or another. If he wanted to be with me, he could find some way to do it, but I wasn't going to try and shake loose what he wanted, what he needed.

Maybe remembering that would bring my mind some peace. I sure as hell hoped so because there was no way I would get any rest as long as I kept having hot dreams about the two of us together.

And if I was going to make this new job work for me, I needed as much rest as I could get.

Chapter Eight

Damian

THE WARM WATER COURSED over the two of us, blurring the lines between our bodies, just like it had back at the bungalow together when she had invited me to join her and had kissed me like I was the only thing that mattered in her life.

Something had happened that had gotten in the way of us for a while, but I seriously couldn't remember what in the hell it was. Something bad, I supposed. Whatever it was, it seemed to have faded away in my memory, and I couldn't remember a damn thing. All I could think about was how much I wished I could have been going down on her right in that moment.

"You feel so good," she murmured to me, so softly that I could hardly hear her above the thundering of the water around us.

She was totally naked, and I ran my hands over her back, over her hips, feeling the shape of her, the curve of her perfect body. Shit, did she know how hot she was to me? I didn't have the words to tell her, but I knew that there were other ways for me to make it clear to her that I just couldn't get enough. And I intended to make sure she understood exactly what was running through my mind in that moment.

I turned her around so that I could watch the water run down the curve of her back in front of me, pooling just above her ass before it ran down her legs and between her thighs, like it was carving a path for me to follow.

I smoothed her hair off her back and kissed down the nape of her neck, over her spine, listening to her breath as it grew a little more needy. This was how I liked her the most, practically pleading with her body, unable to deny how much I turned her on.

I finally reached her ass and knelt down so that I could taste her properly. Pressing my lips to her pussy from behind, I slipped my tongue between her legs and listened to the helpless cry of pleasure that she let out as I teased her.

She arched her back and pushed herself back against me, another moan sliding out of her mouth as I grabbed hold of her ass to pull her onto me a little harder. Fuck, the taste of her was more than I could handle. My cock was straining just to be inside her, and I wondered if she could tell just what she was doing to me.

It didn't take long until she was grinding herself against me, practically riding my face as I extended my tongue and let her use it as she wanted. I would have done anything to give her the pleasure she wanted so badly. She could have asked me to stay there under the running water until I had practically wrinkled up to nothing and washed away, and I would have done it for her. How could I not? There was something so satisfying about pleasing her, something that even pleasing myself didn't even come close to.

She reached behind her and pulled me back to my feet so that my cock was pressed against her pussy once more. The water made her whole body feel as soft and smooth as it possibly could, and it seemed as though I had just been made to slip inside of her. I wasn't going to hold back.

I pushed myself all the way up to the hilt into her pussy at once, filling her, taking her, listening to that cry of pleasure and pressing my mouth to the back of her neck once more.

"Fuck me," she groaned. "Hard. Harder."

I drove myself into her as hard as I could over and over again until I could feel her pussy flexing and clenching around my cock. She turned her head so that we could kiss each other, our mouths starving for one another as she tasted me deeply.

The scent of her pussy must have still been all over my mouth, but she didn't seem to care. Maybe she even liked it. She reached back to clasp my head, her fingers in my hair holding on tight and drawing me in close like she could hardly get enough of me.

I fucked her in long deep strokes, my balls already tingling with the need to find my release inside of her. Her pussy was so perfect—tight, warm, wet, slick, and satisfying—and I forced myself to slow down, not wanting this to be over so quickly, not ready to say goodbye to all of this quite yet.

She purred, and the sound of her pleasure was almost enough to send me over the edge. "You feel so good, baby."

Her voice echoed in my head, a promise of what she wanted me to do to her, and I groaned and pushed harder, like I was trying to make our bodies match once and for all. Somewhere in the back of my mind, I knew something had come between us, but when we were fucking like this, it was hard to remember what that ever could have been.

I could feel myself getting closer and closer to the edge, tipping beyond the point of no return, knowing that I couldn't hold back any longer. But she didn't want me to. I could tell from the way she was grinding back against me that she was ready.

Our bodies were pressed together, reflecting each other, and I pushed harder and harder until finally I felt myself release and—

I snapped back to reality in my bed, staring at the ceiling, having to catch my breath as the sweat that had sprung from every pore clung to the sheets.

Lilah, so close I could almost taste her, could almost touch her. My cock was swollen beneath the sheets, but as soon as it realized she wasn't there, it started to soften once more.

What the fuck had that been about? Okay, I knew in literal terms, but still. I was meant to be getting over Lilah, not letting her get stuck in my head more than she already had. That memory of her was so vivid, it had drawn a whole new encounter to life in my dreams. Lying here now, I just wished it could have been reality.

Fuck, I wanted to touch her again. I needed her, craved her, and wanted her worse than I had ever wanted anyone in my life.

Then I figured out what must have pulled me out of the dream and back to the real world. My phone was buzzing on the table next to me. I grabbed it and checked the time. It was nearly eight in the morning, and I would be late into the office if I didn't leave soon. I took the call without checking who it was, and the last voice I wanted to hear came down the line.

"Damian, what do you think you're doing advertising for another assistant?"

I groaned and rubbed a hand over my face as I heard my mother's question. This was the last thing I wanted to discuss with her, but it was clear that she wasn't going to let it drop until she got an answer.

"What are you talking about?" I asked her, hoping that any remnants of my dream had totally vanished now. I so didn't want to talk to her when I was feeling this way, especially not when she had called me up to berate me about the very woman I couldn't stop thinking about, no matter how hard I seemed to try.

"I saw that you put up an ad for another assistant," she said, her tone accusing like she could hardly believe she had to have this conversation with me.

I had put up the ad the night before after I'd eaten my takeout, determined to get moving away from Lilah and back to something that actually mattered.

"Yeah, I'm taking your advice," I told her. "Finding someone who can help out at the office. I thought you would be happy about it."

"This isn't what I meant and you know it," she said, and she sounded genuinely annoyed that I was making her own plan work against her like this.

"Then what did you mean?" I asked her, sighing heavily, trying not to let my annoyance show in my voice. I knew she was already mad enough without me talking back to her.

"I mean that you should give Lilah another try," she said. "You need to let her back into your life. I think she's good for you."

"Mom, she was my assistant," I reminded her. "Nothing else. Nothing else that someone else can't handle if I put up a job post and start looking."

"She was different," Mom told me, defensive. "You know that. She was good at her job, and she was good for you, too. You'd be silly to let someone like that go."

"I don't think you understand what an assistant actually does, Mom," I told her. "It's not that big of a deal. I just need someone who can work hard and help keep things organized for me."

"You're not going to find someone else like her," she said. "She's good for you, and you know that."

"It sounds like you're talking about more than her being just my assistant," I shot back.

I knew she might have guessed something had happened between us, and I figured the best tactic was to call her on it in the hopes of throwing her off the scent.

"I'm just talking about the assistant work," she replied. "You've been a lot less stressed since she came along. You must have noticed that."

"Yes, but that doesn't mean someone else can't step in and take over," I said. "You really don't need to worry. I'm finding someone else to take the job. You understand that?"

She fell silent. She might have been stubborn, but she knew she had also sown the seeds of that same stubbornness in me, and there was no point arguing when I had already made myself clear.

"Fine," she shot back. "But you should take that down. I know that she'll come back if you ask her. It must have just been a misunderstanding. Nothing more than that. Why don't you try to make it right?"

"Because I have better things to do than run around after a woman who has already made it clear that she doesn't want to work for me," I said a little more sharply than I had anticipated.

"Well, if that's the way you're going to be about it," she said and hung up the phone.

Shit. I knew I was going to have to make up for my harsh words later. I was already pissed at myself for even thinking about Lilah again. Why was it that she was stirring in my memories once more?

I could recall the way she smelled, the way she tasted, the way she sounded when she was close to coming. And the memories of all of those things were enough to keep her fresh in my head, demanding my attention, crying out for just an inch of what I had once had with her.

Staring at the ceiling, I tried to remember what little scraps of the dream I had left. The kiss had been the part that stuck with me the most. She'd kissed me like she had been starving for me and couldn't get enough. That was how I hoped she felt about me, at least. I wanted her to need me. Then maybe I wouldn't feel quite so bad about needing her as much as I did.

Who was this guy? This version of me who seemed to come out of hiding whenever she was anywhere near my head? I didn't know, and I wasn't sure I liked him. He was a whole lot less practical than the other versions of me and probably a lot stupider too.

I didn't like this feeling of being out of control. Normally, that was the only thing I really cared about—having control over my life, my brain, and everything that was going on in both of them.

But now that my father had swung into my business, using my name for shit that I had never agreed to, and now that Lilah was gone and I couldn't get her back, all of that was fucked.

It was over. I was screwed. And I didn't know how the hell I was going to get that control back, given that my own brain seemed determined to work against me with all of this.

That dream was just a reminder of how badly I wanted her back. How much I hoped she felt the same way. I had lost her and let her slip through my fingers, but I had to find a way to move forward from that.

I was bigger than one fuckup. I would learn from this and move forward, and there was no way in hell I was going to let what had happened between us color the rest of my life. Not even the rest of my month or the rest of my day if I had anything to say about it.

This was going to be behind me before I knew it. In just a few weeks, I would be trying to remember her name. If my mom would let me forget it, of course. Maybe I needed to get some distance from her, too, just to make sure she didn't stir up too many memories of Lilah as well.

But for now, I just wanted to get back to reality, as far from that dream as possible. It was going to be difficult to get her out of my head—but I would give it a damn good try.

Chapter Nine

Lilah

AS I MADE MY WAY DOWN the street, I kept my eyes fixed to my phone, making sure I didn't wander past the place I was meant to be getting my sweets from for my sister's baby shower.

I really had no clue at all what I was doing, but I was going to do it well. This weekend was going to be dedicated to making sure I got all the pieces in place and put together to be certain I could pull this off.

My sister and I might not have been close, but that didn't mean I wanted to let her down with this. Quite the opposite actually. I was pretty sure that if I could find some way to pull this off, it might be a way to bridge the gap between us. I hadn't exactly been sister extraordinaire in the time we had both been adults, but there was time to fix that.

Natalie deserved better than me for a sister. Maybe I was getting a little dramatic, but if I had been a little closer with my family, maybe none of this would have happened in the first place. Not the Damian stuff, but feeling so lost after what had happened with my ex.

It had felt like my whole life was spinning out of control, and I was just scrambling to do my best to put all of that back together, knowing that they were going to judge the hell out of me in the process. Perhaps if I had been able to be a little more honest and open with them, I could have relied on them for that support instead of bending over backward to prove I didn't need their help.

I got mad at them inside my head for not doing more to look after me, and then, when the time came, I hadn't even given them the chance. That was hardly playing fair.

What the hell had I done the last time I'd seen them? I had boasted about my new job and made out that I had this amazing life that they should all be jealous of.

I could have been honest with them and admitted that all of this was so new and that I wasn't really sure if I could do it yet, that I wanted to take some time to settle in before I got used to it.

Instead, I had jumped in to make sure they knew just how well I was doing. Because the thought of them looking down on me or judging me again was just way more than I could handle. But that was assuming they would have jumped straight to that. Maybe they would have supported me. Maybe.

That was the attitude I was going into this baby shower with. Building bridges. I needed to get back in touch with the person I had been before all of this had started, before I had started dating my ex, before I had even come to the city.

I still wasn't that old, and I could take the time to put those pieces back together. If I was going to have a little kid in my life, my niece or nephew, I was going to make sure I would be one hell of an aunt to them. Preferably the cool aunt who they came to when they needed advice on stuff that their mom was way too square to give them, right? Yeah, something like that.

In the meantime, I actually had to put this shower together, and I still wasn't sure I had a clue what I was doing.

Cake. That was where I was starting because everyone wanted cake at their parties. I couldn't mess that one up. I hoped not at least.

Oh, shit. I had walked past the street that I was meant to be turning at. I had headed down to this fancy restaurant place in the hopes that they might be able to set me up with a spread, but when I had told them I was putting together the pieces for a baby shower, they had gently suggested I go for a sweet spread instead of a savory on. It was more traditional, they said, and when I indicated that the person I was planning this for was exactly that, the decision was made.

The sweet woman at the restaurant had given me this bakery that she said would be perfect for what I was looking for, and I had decided to take her word for it. I needed to trust people more these days, and I needed all the help I could get when it came to handling something like a baby shower for the very first time.

I was sure I knew the name of the place, but I couldn't place it, so I figured the best course of action was to just go for it, turn up, and hope for the best. I had a budget in mind—Mom had at least offered to help me out with that—and I had no idea if this was going to be way too expensive for me to handle or if it would be a gift from the baby shower gods.

This thing was the whole reason I had run off to California in the first place. I had wanted to get away from all of this, all of the responsibility, all of my certainty that my family saw me as so far behind the rest of them. But now that I was back, now that Damian was out of my life, I didn't see that I had much choice but to dive back into it. And maybe that was a good thing. Maybe I needed to embrace my place in my family. Maybe it had been my ex who had pushed me away from them, and this idea that they wanted nothing to do with me was coming entirely from inside my own head, not from reality. My mom had asked me to help out with all of this, after all. They didn't want to leave me out at least. That had to count for something.

I headed into the bakery and found myself faced with a huge line. Fuck, I was going to be in here for a while. I eyed the display under the glass in front of me and my mouth started to water. I didn't have much of a sweet tooth, but damn, if there wasn't something to be said for the sight of those perfectly crafted cakes in front of me. Some of them looked as though they shouldn't have actually been able to function in our normal earth gravity, beautiful sugary confections that seemed to swell in pastel pinks and blues against the very rules of science.

"Lilah, hello!"

A voice I recognized drew my attention, and I looked over to see a woman I knew standing just beside me at the counter. Melanie. The last person I wanted to see right now.

"Oh, hey," I greeted her, offering her a smile. I hadn't had much time to think about what she had offered me the last time I'd seen her, and honestly, I didn't want to. After that dream I'd had about Damian, I found myself even more confused about the way I felt about him. I wanted to be near him, but I knew that would be admitting I had been wrong to call things off, and I wasn't sure I had the space in my pride for that. No matter how much I missed him.

"What are you doing on this side of the city?" she asked brightly with a big smile on her face. It was hard not to return it. She was so bubbly and sweet.

I wondered how someone like Damian could have come from someone as bright as her or if his moodiness was a response to her attitude.

"Just getting some stuff set up for my sister's baby shower," I replied. "I hope so anyway."

"Well, you've picked the perfect place," she replied. "They have the sweetest little cookies. I was at a party that was catered from here recently, and there were barely any crumbs remaining by the time I left!"

I smiled, hoping that would be the end of the conversation, but I wasn't going to get away that easily. She kept looking at me, then leaned a little closer so she could lower her voice and speak to me a little more privately.

"Now, I don't want to put pressure on you," she murmured, "but I saw that Damian has started looking for a new assistant."

"What do you mean?" I asked, the hairs on the back of my neck standing up.

"I saw that he was advertising for a new assistant," she explained. "I spoke to him about it, but he didn't seem like he wanted to wait much longer to get someone back in that position."

"Right, yeah," I muttered, hoping that my voice was neutral and normal, though I knew that it wasn't. I could feel the tension creeping up into my shoulders already, the weight heavy on my chest.

"I mean, I suppose since he fired you, it's only normal that he would want someone to take that position," she said.

My head snapped up as I narrowed my eyes at her. "What do you mean, fired me?"

She blinked at me for a moment, as though trying to wrap her head around my protest was. "Since the two of you stopped working together," she corrected herself.

Had he told her that he'd fired me? Because that was one hell of a misrepresentation of what had happened. I could already feel a flare of annoyance at the thought of him spinning that story to his mom, especially given how hard I had worked for him while I was there.

When she put it like that, it made it sound as though I had just been incompetent and that he couldn't wait to get rid of me. But I knew better than that.

"Right, yeah," I said, and I tried not to let the annoyance show on my face. I didn't want her to know that I had actually allowed this to bother me. I knew that I should have moved on by now, but the thought of him going around and telling people that he had been the one to get rid of me was galling.

I didn't like that. Not one little bit.

"So, I suppose that if you did want to work for him again, you would have to put yourself back in there soon," she suggested. I knew she was trying to be casual, but her eyes were pinned to me as she waited for a reaction.

"I suppose I would," I replied. I didn't want to give her anything to take back to him. Maybe he was hoping she would run into me so he could pick up on what had been going on in my life. I had no idea if that was the case, but I didn't know if I wanted him to find out that I was hanging around in this place. He knew how much I wanted to avoid doing all this stuff for the baby shower, and he would know that I'd had no other option than to take it on.

Not that I cared what he thought of me at this point. He was my ex-boss, for goodness sake, not my ex-boyfriend. I had nothing to prove to him. Nothing at all. If anything, he had to prove himself to me before I went crawling back to him, given everything that he had done. Given everything that he had fucked up between us and the way he had treated me like I was nothing more than someone who worked for him.

"Maybe worth thinking about," she said.

I nodded. She was still trying to sound casual, but I didn't believe a word of it. This was serious business to her.

"Well, if things with this new job don't work out, I'll think about it," I replied, keeping my voice as icy cool as I possibly could. I didn't want her to catch on to what was going on inside my head. I had no idea if her son had told her what had been happening with us, and I didn't want to be the one to let something slip.

"I think you should," she said.

The woman behind the counter waved to us to get one of us to step forward. She looked harried, annoyed, and I wondered just how many boujee baby showers she'd had to cater in the last few weeks. That was probably the mainstay of her business, and I was about to bring another right to her doorstep.

"Next please!" she announced.

Melanie smiled at me and took a step toward the counter so that she could order. I stood behind her, staring at the floor, trying to wrap my head around what she had just said to me.

Is that really how he thought of me? I couldn't believe it. Did he really think of me as some sort of ex-employee, fired with cause, who he was just trying to replace in the hopes that he would find someone who would do better than I had?

No. If he was advertising for a new assistant already, then he was just doing it to get under my skin because he hadn't wanted someone to work with him in that way in the first place. When I had first been hired, he had been pretty pissed I was there at all, and he wasn't going to go back on that so quickly.

Was he? Or was I just the first step in the change that was coming in him? Perhaps the next woman would be the one to make him into the man I had needed him to be, or the one after that. Maybe I was just the first step in the shift that he needed to make. But even if I was, that didn't mean I was going to sit around waiting for him to catch up with himself, to work out that this was for the best and that he should have switched it up.

Melanie waved goodbye as she headed out of the store, and I offered her a tight smile and waited till the door had shut behind her before I headed toward the counter. I had to focus on this baby shower. That was all that mattered.

"Could you let me know what your catering packages look like?" I asked the woman behind the counter a little more sharply than I initially intended to.

She smiled at me, clearly used to dealing with people with bad attitudes.

"Of course," she replied sweetly.

I tried to relax. I could do this. I could spend the next couple of hours drowning my worries in sugar, and by the time I was done, I wouldn't have any room in my head for anything close to Damian.

Chapter Ten

Damian

COFFEE IN ONE HAND, phone in the other, I strode into the office and promised myself things would go well. I was going to find my new assistant, and nothing was going to hold me back from making sure I got someone else hired by the end of the day.

I headed through the door toward the room I had booked for my interviews today, and I ran into the last person on earth that I wanted to see.

"Mom?" I asked, furrowing my brow as she leaned in the door and waited for me to come in. "What are you doing here?"

She had a habit of sticking her nose into things, regardless of whether I wanted her near them. In some ways, I supposed I could see why my father had been so concerned about her turning up at his wedding out of the blue years ago. Even just to offer commentary on what she thought they should have been doing with the caterer. I knew she meant well, but damn, it was hard not to take it as a comment on the way I was doing things.

I knew she liked Lilah, but it was my choice to move on without her, not my mother's. Sometimes, I felt like I should have invented some department for her to come in and manage, if just to keep her from clogging up my system with all of her dabbling and over-involvement in my life. But even if I did something like that, she would catch on at once, and it wouldn't take long before she got back to reality and started sticking her nose into my business again.

I liked to think I was pretty smart, but I had nothing on my mother and the power moves she could pull if she thought I was daring to go against her advice without consulting her first.

"What, you're saying that I can't come in and visit my own son?" she asked, playing all innocent, but I knew her a damn sight better than that.

I glared at her for a moment and let out a sigh. "And why would you come down here instead of waiting for me at my office?"

She opened her mouth to protest, but there was nothing she could do to convince me of whatever snow job she was about to try on me.

"I just wanted to see how the interviews were going," she replied, casual as hell, as though she hadn't carried out interviews for assistants behind my back not so long ago. "Given that you got rid of the last one I found for you."

"You mean the one I never asked you to find in the first place?" I asked sternly. I had to lay down the law with her. It was the only way she was going to listen to a word that came from my mouth.

But even as I shifted my tone, she just gazed at me like she couldn't wrap her head around what I was saying to her. Like she couldn't tell I was getting pissed.

"Well, clearly you needed her, or else you wouldn't have been bothered about hiring a new one," she shot back, a little triumphant.

Okay, she did have a point there, but that didn't mean I was about to just toss my hands in the air and give up. She didn't get to just turn up here anymore, not after what she had done the last time. Not after she had decided it was just fine for her to invade my life and business with no warning. None of this was fair, and I was going to make sure she didn't get close to my new assistant.

"What have you been doing?" I demanded. "Where are the applicants I called in for an interview today?"

"I suppose they must not have turned up," she replied, practically fluttering her lashes at me in her performance of innocence.

I didn't buy that for a minute. I knew what she had done, and I wasn't afraid to call her out on it. She might have thought she had some power around here, given that I was her son and she was my mother, but she seemed to forget I was the boss when it came to this place, and nothing was going to stop me controlling what happened here.

"Yeah, well, I don't think every single one of them just happened to change their mind at the last minute without telling me," I said.

I headed back over to the reception desk where I knew they were all meant to sign in before they came to speak to me. If she had gotten to them, then she had gotten to them there. Clara, the girl behind the desk, looked up at me nervously as I approached, as though she knew she'd been party to something she shouldn't have done.

"Clara, did you see my mother hanging around here this morning?" I asked.

I could hear Mom's shoes tapping on the polished wood below as she tried to catch up to me, but I had gotten there first. Clara glanced up at me and nodded as though she was giving away some deep, dark secret. She was braced for impact by the time my mom arrived next to me, and I shifted so I could at least take some of the deflection from her pushiness.

"Clara, I thought we said—" Mom said, but I held my hand up to stop her in her tracks. If she really thought she could use my own employee against me like this, then she had another think coming.

"And do you know just what it was she was up to?" I asked.

Clara bit her lip. She looked as though she wanted to vault across the desk and sprint out of there for good. But I wasn't going to get her in any trouble. I knew just how persuasive my mother could be. I had grown up with her, after all.

"I saw her talking to some of the applicants," she blurted out finally. "Before they got a chance to sign in. And when she was done, most of them just left right away."

"What?" I exploded, and I turned to face Mom once more.

She looked like she had been caught with her hand in the cookie jar, a complete inversion of the roles we normally took on as mother and son.

"What were you saying to them?" I asked her.

She managed to smooth away the guilt from her face and pick up where she had left off. "I just told them the truth," she said. "That there's someone else you've settled on for this position. I suppose most of them just didn't want to waste their time."

"I'm going to ban you from this office," I growled at her, but honestly, I was having to hold back an exasperated laugh at how ridiculous this all was.

I could just imagine my mom stalking around the office, ready to pounce on anyone she thought looked like they were applying for a job as an assistant, telling them all the horrible things she could think of about me to keep them away. I didn't know what she had come up with, but there was a part of me that wanted to hear it.

Hell, to them, I was probably some sort of comic book villain now. I didn't even want to imagine what she had told them, but it had been enough to get them all to give up on the hope of an interview with me and get the hell out of there.

"You know that I'm right," she said, scurrying after me as I headed for the elevator that took me to my office. "You know that you want Lilah back and working here."

I fought the urge to roll my eyes at her. "Mom, I told you she's not a good fit here."

"Yes, and you still haven't told me why," she said. "It's all just nonsense, isn't it? I'm your mother. I know you too well for this."

"You know me so well you've been spinning stories to the people who are meant to work for me to make sure they don't turn up at the interview I arranged with them?" I stepped out of the elevator. There was no way in hell I was going to let her try to work this in her favor. I knew her better than that. She might have been able to talk a big game, but I could talk a better one.

"I just told them the truth," she replied, sounding like a pouty teenager. Damn, she could be so ridiculous sometimes.

"You know, some people actually live all the way across the country from their parents," I said to her. "So that they can't interfere with their lives. I think I'm starting to see the appeal of that."

"You don't mean that," she said with confidence.

Sometimes, I was pretty sure there was nobody with a bigger ego than a parent who thought they were doing the right thing for their child. There was just no stopping her, no slowing her down, even when I tried.

"Besides, just think about it," she said. "Lilah could come back to work here. You could stop looking for someone to take her place, and you could focus on your actual work again. That's what you want, isn't it?"

"I thought you hired her because you wanted me to take some time off of work," I said.

She waved her hand as though that was utterly secondary to the point she was trying to make. "You know what I meant."

I stared at her for a moment. How could one woman be so contrary? I didn't know what the fuck I was supposed to do to make her happy, but it seemed like every step I took toward moving on without Lilah, she was there to get in my way. Throwing herself in front of me to make sure I had to slam on the brakes.

"I know what you mean," I said. "But I think you need to get back to your own life now. I have things under control here. Don't you have something better to do than scare away the people I'm supposed to be working with?"

"Better than look out for my son?" she asked. "No. I don't."

"I'm sure you can come up with something," I told her firmly. "Go on. Get out of here before I start actually getting mad about this."

She opened her mouth to protest once more but seemed to think better of it, thank goodness. Instead, she shot me with one last look and turned around to stomp out of there.

She would be annoyed that I hadn't given into her brilliant plan, but I wasn't going to let her run my life any longer. The last time I had given her the space to do that, I had wound up with Lilah in my life, and that had ended up being more trouble than it was worth.

For damn sure.

I picked up the phone and started calling around to the applicants who had been chased out of the building by my mother. Most of them sounded a little shell-shocked that I was calling them at all, and I tried to be as pleasant as possible on the phone so they wouldn't think I was a nutcase or something. No telling what she had told them.

Most of them agreed to meet with me again, thank goodness, and I arranged for us to get together as far from the office as possible—at a little coffee shop on the other side of the city where my mother wouldn't be able to hunt us down like the ruthless mercenary she was.

Eventually, I hung up the phone, satisfied that I had managed to get most of them back on track after the shit my mother had pulled. I was back in the game. That was all that mattered.

I just needed to focus on my books, get everything together, and try to do a little more digging about that missing information. If Lilah had been here, she would have told me to just put it down to bad luck and move on, but she wasn't, so I was stuck with nothing but my own head for company, and that was telling me to go looking for what I had lost.

Or maybe it was her I was craving, somewhere in the back of my mind. I missed her, especially at times like this when I could have used someone to just laugh with at how crazy my mother was being and remind me to chill out every now and then. But she wasn't here any longer, and I had to find some way to deal with that.

I wasn't going to let myself go spiraling into some hopeless back-spin of self-pity. Not when I had been moving forward in the last few days. Lilah was behind me, no matter what my mom might think about the two of us.

Sure, I missed her sometimes, but that didn't mean I couldn't keep going. She was just an assistant at the end of the day, and I could find someone to replace her if I tried hard enough. I didn't need to moon over her. I wasn't that guy. I never had been, and I sure as hell wasn't going to start now.

Forward. That was all that mattered. Maybe I was an asshole for only being able to think about what came next, or maybe this was what I needed to get my head out of my ass and keep my company afloat as my father tried his best to get in the way of it.

I didn't need Lilah to help out or my mom. I didn't need anyone. I had done this alone for long enough, and nothing was going to change that now.

Nothing in the world.

Chapter Eleven

Lilah

I SAT THERE, SIPPING on the oat-milk latte I had made for myself when it had been quiet behind the counter, and closed my eyes for a moment. I could get used to this.

Not that I really should. If I was going to be working there, it wasn't like I was going to be sitting around on my ass drinking coffee and musing on the mysteries of the universe. I would be busting my ass behind the counter to make sure I put the right amount of froth on a cappuccino and stocking up the little gold cookies that came as a side to the coffees.

I still hadn't decided if this was really where I wanted to be working now that the job with Damian was done. His mom had told me to give it a little time, and I did, but I hadn't heard a whisper from either of them and figured that was my sign to move on. I knew there was only a limited amount of time I could spend sitting around trying to figure out what came next before the coffee shop owner went looking for another barista.

The staff seemed pretty chill and they had been helping me get to know the place and figure out how to work the machines so that I wouldn't be totally useless when and if I actually made the jump to working over here.

"Have you ever worked in a place like this before?" Monica, one of the women who worked there, asked me brightly as she quickly frothed up a tub full of milk and used it to top off a few cappuccinos. Her hands moved so quickly it seemed as though she wasn't even pausing for breath.

"No, nothing like this," I admitted. "I don't really know what I'm doing."

"It won't take you long to catch on," she promised me. "It looks more complicated than it is. I promise. Once you get the hang of it, it's pretty self-explanatory."

"Well, that's a relief," I replied as I watched her shake the cocoa powder over the top of the coffees she had just made. She had worked here for a couple of years, and it seemed like she knew how to make most everything work in her favor.

Maybe I would get there one day. Maybe I could get my shit together in a way that actually worked. I had no idea what I was doing here, but perhaps I could be the sage barista handing down advice to the person who needed it most when the time came. It was a shot in the dark, sure, but I had to keep my hopes up.

I hadn't even taken the job there yet. It would only be a matter of time until the big boss started checking her watch and looking for other people, but as long as I was here, keeping my face to the forefront, hopefully, she wouldn't forget me.

I was starting to get pretty nifty with the frother, and I'd even served a couple of pastries to people. Linda, the woman who ran the place, offered to pay me for my time, but I promised her that I wasn't going to start taking her cash until I had actually decided that this was where I wanted to be full time.

Maybe I could make this work. Yeah, I could. I had never worked in a coffee shop before, but then, I had never worked in an office as someone's assistant before I had worked with Damian, and I had made that work.

I could do this. I needed to stop beating around the bush and just take the job. I was lucky that the opportunity had come along so soon. It could have gone so badly for me, leaving me without work for months. But I had walked in here and they had wanted to give me the job. What more could I ask for? I was going to do it.

I picked up my coffee and lifted it to my lips, taking what I hoped was a determined sip, and then—

I looked up and saw Damian walking through the door.

For a second, I thought I must have been dreaming again. The memory of the steamy dream I'd had about him filled my brain all at once, demanding my attention, and it was as though something had wrung me dry. My breath left my chest and I had to grab hold of the table in front of me to keep from tipping over.

Because there was no way in hell that Damian had just walked in here. He scanned the room, and I managed to throw myself behind the counter before he saw me, my heart pounding at a double-time rate in my chest. I didn't want to have to look him in the eye right now, just in case that dream was somehow written all over my face.

Eileen, the woman who was serving at the counter, gave me a funny look, but luckily, he came over and started talking to her before she could ask me what the hell I thought I was doing. I kept my head down and looked around for an escape.

Oh shit. What the hell was he doing here?

As soon as I heard him speak, I knew it was really him. There was no doubt in my mind.

"Hey, can I help you?" Eileen asked him brightly.

"Yeah, could I get a black coffee?" he asked her, his voice a little curt.

I knew he was just distracted—shit, why was I making excuses for him inside my own head right now? He didn't need me to do that. He didn't need me to do anything. And yet, I would always be there, it seemed, to jump and make apologies for his attitude.

Something didn't make sense to me, though, as I crouched down behind the counter and hoped that nobody would notice how fucking strangely I was acting.

Why had he come all the way out here anyway? It was Wednesday, the middle of the work week, and there were coffee shops way closer to the office than this one. Hell, there was actually one inside the building. That was one of the things they had used to sell the very existence of the place to me back when I had first applied. Fully functioning, totally staffed, and exactly where you wanted to get your coffee first thing in the morning. There was no way he had any reason to come all the way down here.

I snuck into the back room so I could get to my feet and watch him through the crack in the door. Okay, had he always been as handsome as that? I felt like my heart was going to come bursting right through my chest, and I was surprised that he couldn't sense the intense mental waves flooding out in his direction as I stood there and watched him.

"Uh, excuse me?"

Barry, one of the other employees, tapped me on the shoulder, and I turned around to see him giving me one hell of a funny look as I lurked in the doorway. I jumped aside so that he could get past, carrying a big sack of coffee grounds out with him.

"Thanks," he muttered, but he seemed pretty thrown by the way I was acting. Shit, so was I.

This was the last thing I had expected. Part of the reason I had gone for this job in the first place was because it was about as far removed as possible from the office I had worked at with Damian and there would be next to no chance of me running into him out here. And yet, he had turned up, as if summoned somehow by the sheer force of my will. I couldn't fucking believe it.

He went to his table, and he gave the waitress a nod of thanks when she brought him his drink. He looked like he was distracted, as though he was waiting for someone. Was he?

I tried to cool my overheated brain, realizing that I needed to calm the hell down. I had no business finding out what was going on here. He was just minding his own business and going about his life.

Just then, a woman walked through the door and into the coffee shop to join him.

He got to his feet as soon as he saw her. I snuck out from behind the door and hustled to a spot behind the coffee machine where I knew he couldn't see me.

The woman he was standing for was dressed smartly, like she had just come from the office herself. She looked a little younger than him, with a tight coil of blonde hair at the back of her head and a pale pink lipstick that washed her out a little. Or was I just hoping that it did because I was being a bitch? I had no idea.

He didn't give her a hug or a kiss, but the smile he offered her seemed warmer than it had to be for something casual. He took her back over to the table, and I kept my eyes pinned to them as they seemed to chat a little. She laughed at something he said, a little too loudly, as though she was trying to impress him. I felt my stomach twist inside of me. I wished that it could have been me instead.

Or that the dream I'd had about him coming into this place before could have actually come true. If I could only reach out for him and tell him I was here and that seeing him in person only made me miss him more than I ever thought possible.

Before I could hide again, the woman had approached the counter—and I realized I was the only person standing behind it. She didn't bother to greet me. instead, she pointed to the pastry display next to me.

"Is that an apricot Danish?" she asked.

I blinked at her for a moment and just stared. Where had all my words gone? I was sure I had been able to speak before she had turned up.

"Uh, yes," I finally blurted out.

"And could I get it without the glaze, or does it only come with it?" she pressed. She had brown eyes, and when she smiled at me to try and prompt me to answer, it didn't reach them.

"It comes with it," I replied.

She sighed and tapped her nails on the counter in front of us. They were long and perfectly crafted, painted a pale pink to match her lips. I clenched my fists so that my own bitten-down nubs wouldn't show. I didn't need any more reason to feel bad about myself right now.

"Okay, I'll try one of them," she replied.

I went to pick up the tongs to get it for her, and she sighed.

"No, actually, just a croissant. The sweet one, not the savory." She didn't bother to apologize.

I was judging her, even though I knew I shouldn't. Maybe she was just nervous? Maybe she was just the kind of person who didn't feel the need to trip over herself to be nice to service workers.

I got her the croissant. She paid and didn't leave a tip. I watched as she went back over to the table, offering Damian a huge, dazzling smile as she did so. This one had no trouble reaching her eyes. Which meant that it must have just been me she didn't want to talk to.

I retreated a little behind the counter, making sure that Damian couldn't see me, and watched as the two of them chatted with one another. They seemed excited to catch up on everything that had happened, both of them nodding and listening intently as though this really mattered. I wished that I could have made out what they were saying, but at this distance, I couldn't hear a word. If I got any closer, I would give away the fact that I was right here and listening in to my ex taking his new girl out on a date.

I had no idea he would move on so quickly. I supposed we had never officially been together, but I was still stinging from the way things had ended. I had assumed he'd feel the same way, but no, he was already out with someone else, already chatting it up like he had known her all her life.

And she seemed uptight to say the least. Maybe I'd just gotten the wrong side of her, but she seemed rude and entitled, and she didn't even have the decency to leave a tip. Was that really the kind of woman he wanted to be with? Evidently, it was.

Shit, I was going to give myself a complex. I needed to get out of there before I spent another second overthinking all of this. I was getting pissed off just watching the two of them together, and I was mad as hell that I was allowing this to get to me.

This was meant to be my place, a place I could come and just relax without stress, and yet, I had allowed myself to get all spun up just because some guy I used to sleep with happened to have rolled up with the new girl he was dating? Yeah, that wasn't what I needed right then.

But even still, it hurt. It hurt like a motherfucker, even though I knew I should have been over it. I'd never had a claim on this guy, so why was I letting him get to me now?

I needed to get myself under control. I needed to get my life in hand. I needed to get the hell over him, and I wasn't going to be able to do that as long as I was hanging around and watching him on some hot date with the new girl he was seeing.

I ducked back behind the counter and told myself I could get out of there as soon as they were gone. I just didn't want him to see me. Not yet. Not so soon.

Not when I didn't have my walls up.

Chapter Twelve

Damian

AS SOON AS I SAW HER walk through the door, my heart sank.

Motherfucker. My father had promised me that he was going to make this right, and all he had done was send out someone he thought could distract me from my task. Bullshit. I wasn't going to let this happen.

He had called the office a few days before, offering to meet up so that the two of us could talk about what had happened while I had been away in California. I had been foolish enough to be cautiously optimistic. Maybe he was going to make it right, after all this time. Maybe he was going to fix the mess that he had made.

When he had suggested coming down to this coffee shop, I assumed he must have been paying attention. This was where I had done the interviews for my new assistant, after all, and he clearly wanted me to be comfortable wherever he sent me.

I should have known then that he was trying to set the tone to make sure I wouldn't get too suspicious. I should have known it was too damn good to be true. I knew him better than that, but apparently, I was still foolish enough to fall for whatever it was he was trying to sell me.

Shit, I should have insisted he be the one who came down here to the office and that if I didn't see him in person, I would consider that an official announcement he was moving forward without my consent.

Instead of coming to meet with me himself, he had sent out his own assistant, Tamsin, to take care of the task. I had met her a couple of times before when I had stopped by the office, and I had always noticed the way she looked at me as though she wanted to take a bite out of me, and not in a good way. Her shirts always seemed to be cut just a little lower than they needed to be, and it was obvious that my dad hadn't hired her just because of her killer skills on the job.

Judging by the big smile she produced as soon as she saw me, she had been told to put on a bit of a show to make sure I paid attention to everything she had going for her.

"Damian, it's so good to see you," she greeted me, giving me a big hug as soon as she arrived at the table.

I pulled back from her at once. What did she think she was doing? She smelled of cheap flowers, a body spray I couldn't place, but it made me think of an eighth-grade dance.

"Where's my father?" I asked her.

She shrugged. "He thought I would be perfectly qualified to share everything you need to know about this deal," she told me, the smile not wavering from her face for a moment.

Now I was seriously getting mad. No matter how qualified she might have been for her job, my father should have come down here himself to prove to me that he was actually serious about this. I wouldn't have put up with this treatment from anyone else that I worked with, and just because he was my father didn't mean I had to put up with it from him.

I didn't know what my father had said to her, but it was clear she was going to stick to it as best as she could. I got the feeling it had something to do with hitting on me in the hopes I wouldn't notice what a mess he was making of the business right now.

Yeah, well, I had bigger things on my mind than that, and I hated to break it to him, but I was never going to be the son he could bribe with pretty girls. That was where we diverged, I suppose. If I had sent a pretty girl along to a meeting with him, he would have been putty in my hands in ten seconds flat. But I didn't work that way. Never had, never would. He needed to get that through his thick skull, or else there was going to be some serious trouble.

"I'm not interested in forming any kind of deal," I told her firmly. "I just want to establish that I'm not going to have anything to do with my father's business."

"I'm sure you'll want to rethink that once you've taken a look at what we have to offer," she continued, her voice so irritatingly perky that I could hardly handle it.

The top two buttons on her shirt were undone. Was that something my father had offered in the hopes of getting me to agree to all this? He really didn't know me at all if he thought I would fall for a thing like that. It made me a little sick to think of him telling her to put on this show for me, hoping that it would get me to give in to whatever he wanted me to do.

"No, I won't," I replied bluntly.

She rose to her feet once more. There was a flicker in her face, an irritation impossible to hide. Maybe she had been told this was going to be easy. Maybe my father had truly believed it would be. I had no idea, and, frankly, I wasn't interested in finding out. I just wanted this to be over already so I didn't have to sit through another moment of this appallingly awkward and totally useless so-called meeting.

"I'm going to get something to drink," she replied. "Can I get you anything?"

"I'm fine," I muttered, and I watched as she headed up to the counter.

Fucking hell. Did he really think this was going to work? That he could dangle someone like her in front of me and I would just give up on what I had been sticking by all this time and act like nothing had happened between us?

Tamsin didn't know what she was getting herself into. My father had probably told her that this was going to be easy, that she could make something like this quick for herself—and that she could make sure this was over soon enough and that she wouldn't have to worry about that for another moment, not if she could avoid it.

But I wasn't going to let him throw me off the scent that easily. I knew what he was trying to do, and it might have worked on the creepy guys his own age that he kept around, but I wasn't a dude who got distracted just because there was a hot girl in front of me.

That was when I saw her.

As I watched Tamsin at the counter, chatting with the woman on the other side, it took me a moment to realize where I had heard that voice before. It was familiar. Something about it sent a shiver down my spine, as though my body was reacting to her nearness again. When my eyes focused on who it was, it felt like my stomach had dropped into my shoes.

Lilah? There was no way that could be her, but there was no mistaking that bright red hair, those green eyes, and that smile she gave Tamsin as she took her order.

My jaw dropped. How long had she been working here? What were the chances I had just booked a meeting at the very place she worked at now? Had she spotted me here, or was she just pretending as best she could that she couldn't see me to avoid any more awkwardness?

Her eyes slid over to mine, and I knew she had spotted me. Suddenly, this stupid meeting with Tamsin was the last thing on my mind.

Tamsin was taking a long time to order, and it seemed as though Lilah was having a hard time being courteous and keeping her cool, but she wasn't letting it show on her face. Unless you knew her well, like I did, you would never have guessed there was anything up with her.

I knew she could feel me looking at her, and I wondered if she felt that same rush being so close to me again that I did now that she was near and I knew it.

Eventually, Tamsin seemed to get frustrated, and she gave up and strode back to the table, shaking her head as though she expected me to just go along with her attitude.

"I can't believe some of the people here," she muttered, glancing back and shooting a hard look at Lilah.

I was already completely beyond even pretending to have any interest in her. How could I when the woman I hadn't been able to get out of my head for so long was standing right there in front of me, as though the universe had just gifted her back to me?

"What are you doing here?" I asked Lilah, not sure how else to start that conversation.

She stared at me for a moment, eyebrows raised.

"I work here," she replied, tightening the forest-green apron that was wrapped around her waist as though it was some protective armor she had put on to fight me off.

"And before you ask, yes, I've seen the last few dates you've been on," she shot back.

Dates? It took me a second to figure out what she was referring to, but then it hit me. She must have seen the interviews I'd had with the women who had applied for the assistant job. How long had she been here without me noticing? Without saying anything? Without at least letting me know that she was around?

"They weren't dates," I said.

She shook her head and held her hand up. "Hey, I'm not here to judge." The way she said it totally contradicted what had just come out of her mouth.

"Yeah, and you wouldn't have any right to, either," I fired back, more defensive than I needed to be.

"I didn't say I would," she replied.

I could sense Tamsin standing behind us, probably wondering what the hell was going on and why I was acting so harshly toward some random barista I had never seen before.

"Well, then, we're in agreement," I replied.

She narrowed her eyes at me for a moment, as though trying to come up with something cutting that would put me in my place. She could try, but I was already prepared to shoot back at her. Today had already been a letdown, and if someone wanted to come in and frustrate me even further, then they were going to have to find their own way to deal with my reaction.

"Are you going to order something?" she asked.

"I'll pay for it," Tamsin replied, jumping in at once, totally not sensing the vibe that should have been evident. Shit, I would need to tell my father that he should be more careful who he chose for this assignment because she wasn't doing much of a job at all. Surely, there had to be better qualified candidates out there to take care of all of this.

"You don't have to do that," I told her.

She stepped forward, as though she wanted to make sure she wasn't being upstaged by another woman.

"I really don't mind," she replied, lowering her voice like the words were just meant for me.

I ignored her. I wasn't going to play this game. Not a chance in hell. I could feel my blood boiling in my veins. The anger that had started bubbling as soon as I had seen Tamsin walk through the door was more than I could take. I knew I shouldn't have been taking it out on Lilah, but the sheer shock of seeing her again when I hadn't been ready to had sent me spinning.

"I think it's more traditional for the man to pay for the date, isn't it?" Lilah said, her voice icy. "Though I would think that you would usually go for somewhere a little more impressive than a coffee shop."

"Stop talking to me like that," I told her bluntly. I could have been more polite, but then so could she.

I had known I wasn't going to be able to avoid her forever. Eventually, the two of us were going to come crashing into one another again. But I had never expected it to go like this. Not really. Not now. Not so soon after we had been wrapped up in each other, when we had been holding on to each other so tight I was sure I would never be able to let her go.

Damn, I missed that. Even as she stood there on the other side of the counter from me, looking as though she didn't have a nice thing to say in her head, I missed that.

"If you're not going to order anything, you'll need to step out of the line," she told me, taking control of what little power she had in this situation to make sure I didn't get the better of her. "I can't have you holding up other customers."

"There aren't any other customers here," I pointed out.

She narrowed her eyes at me. "So are you going to order or not?" She raised her voice a little as though daring me to throw something back at her.

Before I could, someone emerged from a door behind the counter. "Lilah, is everything all right?" the older woman asked Lilah.

Lilah glanced over at her as though she had been caught in the act. Before I could say or do anything else, Lilah ripped off the apron she had been wearing and pushed it into the hands of the woman I presumed she was working for.

"I need to get out of here," she blurted out.

She strode around the counter and out of the door—leaving a heavy silence in her wake. And me wondering what the hell I was meant to do next.

Chapter Thirteen

Lilah

AS SOON AS I MADE IT out on to the street, I let out a deep, shuddering breath that I didn't realize I had been holding—and I wanted to curse myself for what I had just done.

I couldn't believe I had walked out of that job. Holy shit. What the hell had I been thinking? I had no idea what was running through my mind, but I knew I couldn't go back.

Damian. Fucking Damian. As soon as he dropped back into my life, it felt like everything just went flying. When he was close to me, I was unable to keep myself together. When I had seen him with that other girl, I should have been cooler, should have been calmer, but it wasn't like I could just forget everything we had done together the way he seemed to be able to.

I stood outside one of the shopfronts across from the coffee shop I had just walked out of and stared at myself in the reflection. I couldn't go back now. They wouldn't want me back, even if I went in there and begged for another chance. I didn't deserve another shot.

I stormed off down the street, and I could feel tears pricking my eyes. He still had that power over me. I hated that. I hated that I allowed him to have that control, even though I had been the one to walk away.

My phone sprang to life in my pocket, and I grabbed it at once, hoping that it would be something to take my mind off what was going on inside my head. Sure enough, as soon as I lifted it to my ear, my head dropped the panic and turned to amusement instead.

"Lilah, hello!" a voice exclaimed to me.

"Melanie?" I asked. I couldn't believe she had managed to get hold of me again. She always seemed to pick the perfect moment to slide into my life again, when I just needed someone to get my mind off what was going on.

"Yes, it's me," Melanie replied. "Could you come by Damian's office right now? I'd like to talk to you."

I took a deep breath. Well, it wasn't like I had anywhere else to be right now. And at least I knew I wasn't going to run into him back there, since I had just walked out on my job, leaving him behind on his date.

"What for?" I asked, more than a little cautious.

"I'll tell you when you get here," she replied. "Do you want to come down and meet with me? There is plenty that I'd like to share with you."

"Sure," I replied, rubbing my hand over my face. "Why not? I'll be there in half an hour."

"Wonderful," she replied, and I could hear the smile in her voice.

Despite myself, I couldn't help but return it. "I'll see you soon," I told her, and I hung up the phone and started to walk.

I would have to book it to get there in the half hour I had promised her, but I could do it. Besides, I needed something to take my mind off what the hell I had just done. I needed to get out of there before the reality of it hit me too hard.

By the time I got to his office, Melanie was looking at her watch, and she beamed when she saw me. It felt strange being back there, as though I was invading a space I shouldn't have been in. Some place from my past that didn't belong to me anymore.

"Lilah, so wonderful to see you," Melanie told me, and she gave me a quick hug that caught me off guard.

I hadn't been ready for such kindness. It was more than I had expected. Suddenly, I felt a wash of tears threaten to rise up and through me, and I had to do my best to keep them under control as she pulled back.

"So, I'm assuming since you're here that you still haven't found a job?" she asked.

I opened my mouth, not sure how to respond. Well, truthfully, I had found a job, but I had also fucked it up beyond all belief to boot.

I shook my head. "I haven't got one yet. The coffee shop didn't work out."

"Well, you don't have to worry about that," she told me, waving her hand. "I know I can get you back in here. Damian is looking for a new assistant, but you know that he doesn't actually like the part where he has to meet new people, does he?"

"I suppose not," I said, managing a slight smile. It stung to think of him, to remember him on such intimate terms. I had tried so hard to put all of that out of my head, but I couldn't hide from it any longer. I wanted to forget him, to forget everything that we had been through together, but I couldn't. No matter how hard I tried.

"He's interviewing for someone else to take the position," she warned me. "If you want to get back to the office, you're going to need to make a move for it soon."

"I don't—I don't know if I want that," I confessed. I felt torn. I should have been jumping for any position that came my way, but how was I meant to do that when I wasn't sure I could so much as stand to be in a room with this guy again?

"He's not going to wait long," she told me. "I hope you know that."

"I do," I shot back, a little defensive. "But it's not my—I mean, he didn't even want an assistant when he hired me. I don't see why he would be looking for another one so soon."

"Because you left him in the lurch," she replied. "You did a good job and you made his life easier, and then you just took off and left. He wasn't going to wait around after that, now was he?"

"I guess not," I admitted. I hadn't thought about it like that, that I had made things easier for him and that he wanted to have that back. My emotions were so wrapped up in everything that had happened between us that I'd hardly had time to think about the fact that I was meant to be working with him, too.

"I tried to keep him from interviewing anyone else, but he's stubborn, and he's going ahead with it," she replied, shaking her head with a sigh. "How much longer do you think you'll need?"

"I don't know," I replied, bristling slightly. I was being tugged in so many directions at once, and I didn't know which one I was meant to take. It just didn't feel fair or right. I needed space to figure this out for myself, but no answers were coming.

"I need time to think," I told her. "Can you give me that?"

"I don't know how much longer I'm going to be able to hold him off from making a choice," she warned me. "But I'll do what I can. All right?"

"Alright," I muttered. If Damian knew I was here, he would probably get mad at his mother all over again. I didn't even know myself why she seemed so set on pulling me back into his life. It seemed like there was some reason she thought I was good for her son, even if she wasn't totally clear on why herself.

"I suppose you'll want to get out of here before he gets back," she told me.

I nodded. "I don't think I should be here."

"Well, get used to it," she replied cheerfully. "Since you're going to be back at work here soon enough."

I had to laugh. Her optimism was infectious, and even though I'd had one hell of a day, I couldn't help but smile at how bright she was being.

"Fair enough," I conceded.

I turned to walk the distance back to my apartment. When I got home, Violet was already there, and I practically flopped onto the couch with exhaustion as soon as I got through the door.

"You okay?" she asked.

I let out a groan. I didn't want to have to run through all of it again, but if anyone deserved to hear it, she did. I filled her in from the top down, about seeing Damian at the coffee shop, about walking out of my job there, about seeing his mom back at the office once more.

"Sounds like you had one hell of a day," she muttered. I nodded. "Wine?"

"Badly needed," I said.

She went to pour me a glass. When she sat down on the couch next to me, she eyed me for a moment, then came out with it.

"So what are you going to do?" she asked.

"About the job?" I asked.

She nodded. "About the job."

"I don't know," I admitted. "I mean, what do you think I should do about it?"

"I know that being around him is tough," she replied with a sigh. "But it paid well. And it seems like you've got his mom on your side, at least. That has to count for something."

"Yeah, I suppose so," I said.

She nodded. "And besides, she's right. You did kind of leave him in the lurch, even though you had good reason to."

"This is why they tell you never to get involved with someone you work with," I said. "It just turns into a huge mess, doesn't it?"

"Seems that way," she replied, making a face. "Or maybe that's just you."

"Hey, are you suggesting that I'm messy?"

She shrugged. "Well, you're the one dealing with all of this," she teased. "Seems like the sort of thing not everyone could pull off."

"I should have walked away from that job as soon as I found out it wasn't what I was applying for," I groaned. "I only have myself to blame for this."

"I think he deserves a little bit of the blame, too," she said. "Hey, do you think he was just interviewing those women that you saw him with at the coffee shop? Maybe it wasn't like you thought at all."

"Nah, the one that I saw him with today, it was really obvious there was something going on between them," I replied, grimacing. "The way she hugged him and stuff—it didn't look professional at all."

"Well, then I guess you don't have to worry about anything getting in the way of you doing your job," she pointed out. "If he's seeing other people, then you're safe. Right?"

"Yeah, right," I said, chewing my lip nervously. She had a point. Technically, if he was dating other people, then I didn't have to concern myself with my feelings for him.

But I didn't know if I could handle being around him, knowing that there was no chance for us to be together. Because even now, I missed him like hell.

"I think you're going to need another glass of wine," Violet suggested and she got to her feet to grab me another glass to get me through the rest of the evening.

I was so thankful she was there to help me because if I'd had to deal with all of this myself, I wasn't sure I would have been able to keep my head. It felt like it was stuffed full of more than I could handle, and frankly, I just wanted to forget that all of this had happened.

But I was in the real world now, and the real world wouldn't let go of me so easily.

Chapter Fourteen

Damian

"THANKS FOR COMING IN," I told Hannah, one of the other applicants that I had just finished interviewing.

We shook hands at the door, and I kept the smile on my face right up until it closed behind her. As soon as she was gone, I slumped into my seat and pondered everything that had happened today.

I couldn't believe Lilah had been at that coffee shop. And I couldn't believe I had just let her walk out of there without chasing her down. Where the hell had she been going? Had she come back afterward?

I had scheduled a few interviews, which I shifted back to the office to avoid running into her again. I wouldn't be able to keep my head in the game if I was so distinctly aware of her presence in the room with me.

The interviews had gone as well as I could have hoped, but nobody made me feel like they were right for the job. They were qualified, but they just seemed a little robotic. I couldn't help but think of the first time I had met Lilah, when she had stood up out of her seat to tell me off for interrupting her interview. I had known in the back of my mind I had to hire her on the spot, even if I didn't want to accept it at that moment. But none of them had that nerve, that courage. I needed that. Someone who could stand up to me.

Or maybe I just needed her.

I had been on edge ever since Tamsin had left the meeting we'd had together earlier that day—if you could call it that. She was really just flirting, trying to wheedle me into seeing things from my father's perspective so he could get me where he wanted me. I was colder to her than I needed to be, but I wasn't going to put up with his shit, and I sure as hell wasn't going to let him think that any of this had worked on me.

I needed to speak to him, but I had called the office a couple of times and hadn't gotten anything in return. He was avoiding me. I was just waiting for Tamsin to get back to the office so she could tell him to his face that his plan had failed and that I hadn't gone along with his bullshit idea to get me to do what he wanted.

He was avoiding me. And now Lilah was avoiding me too. I didn't know what I had done to make this mess so bad, but it seemed like the only life I got to live was one that was mostly this screaming disaster. I felt like all of it was out of my control, but that was far from the truth. I knew this was my fault. I had taken my eye off the ball when I had been away, and this was how the universe responded. With punishment. By reminding me that I shouldn't ever dare do it again.

I should have taken note the first time the files went missing from my office. That should have been the first hint that I wasn't paying close enough attention. Hell, looking back, maybe it had even been Lilah who'd gotten rid of them. It wouldn't have made a whole lot of sense, since she had been the one to help me put them back together again, but at this point, nothing in my life made a whole lot of sense. Why shouldn't that have been the truth?

It had been chaos enough as it was. Maybe I just needed to embrace the fact that I couldn't trust anyone right now. Not even the one person I was sure I could actually believe in.

Shit, I hated this. It felt like my whole life had been falling apart since I had returned from California—since the last time Lilah and I had been together. Not that it had anything to do with that, of course. No chance in hell.

My phone buzzed on my desk, and I answered it at once. Anything that would keep my head off Lilah for the time being.

"Hello?"

"I just heard from Tamsin." My father's voice came down the line. He had his big-boy tone on, like he was actually going to dare to tell me off, even though he must have known he didn't have any right to do it.

"What do you think you were playing at, talking to her like that?" he asked.

"What are you talking about?" I fired back. Was he really going to get mad at me right now? That asshole. He was the one who had made this mess for himself and the woman he'd pulled into it. He could sit there and find some way to handle it.

"I'm talking about the fact that you brushed her off even though she came all the way down there to meet with you after I'd had an emergency come up," he said.

Oh, come on. If he was going to spin me a lie, was that really the best he could come up with?

"An emergency?" I snorted with disdain. "Let me guess. Did this emergency have something to do with a tropical island? Probably one filled with girls in bikinis?"

"I know you don't think I spend my time doing anything serious," he snapped back. "But maybe you need to accept that I just have a different way of doing things than you."

"Oh, I do accept that," I told him hotly. I shouldn't have been letting him get under my skin, but damn, that was hard when all this anger felt like it was swelling up to consume me. I wanted him to know how much he'd hurt me with this mess he had dragged my business into. As though he didn't already know damn well.

"I just need you to accept that there's nothing for me to gain from you using my name when you're trying to close deals, you understand?" I told him firmly. That was the end of it. I wasn't going to hear anything else from this guy. He really thought he could sit there and tell me how things were meant to be done?

"Maybe you need to think about doing things differently," he suggested, but I could tell he didn't much care if I took his advice or not. He just wanted to get one over on me.

I could have been nothing but sweetness and light to that girl, and he would have still come at me with this attitude because I hadn't gone along with what he had demanded of me. And that made him so mad I was surprised he could handle himself.

"And what exactly do you mean by that?" I asked him. I tried to keep my voice steady, but it was difficult when I just wanted to tell him he needed to fuck off out of my life and out of my business. My brain hurt. How did he think any of this was okay?

"You could actually listen to my assistants when they meet with you," he replied. "Did you like Tamsin? Because you treated her like—"

"I treated her like anyone else you would have sent down there," I told him firmly. I knew that, to him, being anything other than a slavering creep over a pretty girl was basically the equivalent of kicking her under a car, but the same didn't go for me. She was just business as far as I was concerned, and I wanted to keep her that way.

"I wasn't there to flirt, Dad. I was there to get the job done. I'm sorry you can't seem to accept that."

"You—you need to listen to me," he told me, and there was an edge of desperation to his voice, like he knew I was slipping away from him.

"You could have told me all this in person," I said. "I can come down to your place right now if you want to try. How about it?"

"Fine," he told me.

I hung up and got to my feet before he could change his mind. In five minutes, he would call me back and tell me no, actually he hadn't meant it. That really, it wasn't that big a deal at all and we could work it out over the phone.

Because he knew as soon as we were face to face, I would tear him a new asshole and make sure he never dared to talk that kind of shit to me again. He might have been my father, but that didn't mean I was about to roll over and just let this happen.

I could feel anger pulsing through me, and I knew I should have known how to control it better by now, but I couldn't stop myself. I wanted to hear him say that to my face. He couldn't just send his girls down to try and charm me. If he had something to say to me, then he could say it with me standing in front of him.

Though I knew he would duck and dive to avoid that as soon as I was actually in front of him. That was how he always worked, talking a big game and then sliding away from his responsibility when he got the chance.

I got down to his office, and he was there waiting for me as though the two of us were a couple of teenagers ready to throw down after school. That was what he made me feel like sometimes—like I was a kid again, making more trouble for him than he needed.

He pointed through to his office. "Right this way," he told me. "And if you can avoid being rude to any of my staff on the way there, I'd appreciate it."

I clenched my jaw to avoid shooting back a snarky response. Who did he think he was? Fucking asshole. He was the one who had gotten himself into this mess, and he could talk himself out of it if he wanted. If he could.

"So are you here to apologize to Tamsin?" he asked as soon as the door was shut behind us.

I rolled my eyes. He was the one who had come up with the bright idea to send her out there in the first place.

"I think you should be the one apologizing to her," I fired back. "You sent her out there when you know you should have dealt with it yourself."

"I wanted you to speak to someone else for a change," he told me, dropping the excuse he'd been trying to throw at me to make me believe he'd actually had an emergency that had kept him from coming out.

"And maybe actually treat a woman the same way you would a man, huh?" he added, knowing that would push my buttons since I hated the way he treated women. The way he had always seen it, I was the one doing something wrong by not using them as bait.

"Oh, don't try to play that card with me," I warned him. "I know you too well for that. I'm not the one who keeps women around as fucking window dressing."

He bristled—and I knew that I had stepped over a line, but frankly, at this point, I didn't care. He had taken my name, the name of the business I had worked so hard to put together, and he had tried to use it for his own benefit. I didn't owe him shit. Not one fucking thing. I wasn't going to allow him to use me anymore, and if he thought throwing some pretty girl in my direction was going to fix things, he had another think coming.

"You don't know what you're talking about," he told me, his voice low and pissed.

I was so beyond the point of trying to be nice to him by now. I had given him every opportunity to come and talk this over with me properly, where we could thresh out the details and do what was right for both of us, but he had skipped out on that. The time for decency had passed. He stood there in front of me, this little man, and I could have laughed at how fucking pathetic he looked. How could he look at himself in the mirror?

"Oh, I think I do," I replied. "Because every time I come to your place, you seem to have them draped around for anyone to look at. You think that's what respect looks like?"

"They choose to—" he started, but I was already way ahead of him on this one.

"They choose to because you have the money to make it worth their while," I reminded him. "Do you really think it's your glittering personality they are hanging around for?"

His face got a little darker. I could have held back, but I was in it now, and nothing was going to stop me. He wasn't going to stand there and act like he had any amount of respect for women when he was willing to toss them out in front of me and use them as bait when he was too scared to face up to the mess his own mistakes had left behind.

"You have to use my name to get anywhere in this business," I said. "What makes you think they're seeing you as such a success that they just can't resist you?"

"Oh, for once, get the fuck down off your high horse," he finally exploded back at me. "You've always looked down on me, just because I actually want to have fun with my money instead of sitting around acting like a dragon and hoarding it. How do you think that feels?"

"I'm the one with a business that actually works," I said. "And you're the one dragging my name up because you know that nobody's going to take you seriously if you don't. I think I know what side I would rather be on."

"You never bothered to listen to me," he muttered, and I could tell that I was starting to get under his skin. Good. He had been pissing me off all month long, and I didn't see why he should get away with treating me so badly when I had tried to give him the chance to work through this together.

"You never bothered to reach out to me to try," I said. "I do things differently, and they work for me. If you have a problem with that, then you should say it to my face instead of sending girls out to do your job for you because you think I'm going to be stupid enough to fall for them the way you do."

"You should have some respect for me," he warned. "Because—"

"Because, what? You're already dragging my name through the mud." I was more pissed than ever now. "It's not like I got a choice in that. I don't see why I should respect you when you don't give a damn about how you come off to me or the people I work with."

"Because I'm your father," he spat back, like he thought he really had any power over me any longer.

He had been my father my whole life, and he had never given me any reason to respect him. He had always been playing away from home, always had his eye on the next woman, never seeming to figure out they were all just with him because they wanted his money, not because they adored his personality. I had seen him make the same mistakes over and over again, and now he wanted me to act like I had never seen any of that happen in the first place? Bullshit. Nobody knew his bad sides better than I did.

"And I'm your son, but that doesn't seem to stop you from doing whatever you want with my name," I said angrily. "You really think I'm going to listen to you for any of this? For advice on how to make this better when all you've ever done is make things worse?"

He opened his mouth to protest, but I turned before he could say a word. I didn't have anything else to say to him, and anything I came out with was just going to sour things even further. I needed to work off some tension right now. And there was only one place I could think of where I could do that the way I wanted to—the driving range. I was going right there, and I wasn't going to let anything slow me down. I needed a break.

Preferably from the whole of reality.

Chapter Fifteen

Lilah

"I JUST DON'T UNDERSTAND that guy," I moaned to Violet as I picked up my breakfast toast to take a bite of it. Then I thought better of it. I wasn't even hungry.

I didn't know why I was pretending I wanted to eat. I couldn't think about anything but the mess going on inside my head right now. The mess that was all because of a certain guy who I couldn't seem to get the hell out of my life.

"I think you're the one you need to understand right now," Violet replied. She took a sip of her coffee and stared at me for a moment.

I knew she was right, but damn, that was the last thing I wanted to hear right now.

"What do you mean?" I asked. I had tossed and turned all night long, unable to stop thinking about the man who just seemed to refuse to get out of my head.

"I mean, you're going back and forth with this guy," she pointed out. "You won't take the job back, but you won't move on, either. It seems like you're hoping that something's going to change, and then you can just be with him again."

"That's not what I'm hoping for," I replied, but I couldn't argue against what she had said.

Melanie had basically just dropped a few hints that she might be able to get me back in the door with Damian, and I had been willing to pass up a perfectly good job at the coffee shop, storming out the first chance I got.

I had called them up earlier this morning, but after the back and forth and then my eventual acting out for no apparent reason, they had asked me not to come back. Which I firmly understood. I wouldn't have let me come back to work there either.

"Then why aren't you back out there looking for a job?" she asked. "What are you waiting for? It doesn't make sense."

"It makes sense," I said, even though I knew she was right. I just didn't know how to make myself get up and pick up where I had left off.

I wanted to be able to make things right. I wanted to be able to go back to reality, but how the hell was I meant to do that when it felt like I couldn't figure out how to move forward from any of this?

"You need to either take that job with Damian or get out there and start putting in more applications," she told me bluntly.

I knew that she was right. Damn, she was so fucking right it hurt a little bit. She had been putting up with me for a long-ass time, letting me stay here even though I hadn't always been working, and now I had walked away from two jobs within a month. No wonder she was worried about me.

If I had been in her position, I would have been too. She probably thought I was going to spend the next month lazing around, feeling sorry for myself. I liked the idea of that, but I had to prove to her I was still willing to put up a fight to stay here with her.

"I know, I know," I said. "I just don't know if I can go back and work for him, you know? If he's dating someone else and all that."

"You don't even have to stay there for long," she urged me. "Just as long as it takes to find yourself another job. His mom wants you back there, and it seems like she's got some sway over the situation. Why not take advantage of that?"

I chewed my lip. Okay, so maybe I could do that. Maybe I could work there just for a little bit. But what if I found myself falling for him again? What then? I had no idea what the hell I was meant to do with myself, being so close to him, knowing that I couldn't get involved.

I was terrible at denying myself what I wanted, even more so when it was something I knew I wasn't meant to have. He might have been an asshole, but there was no denying the chemistry between us—well, the chemistry between us when he was being the decent version of himself at least.

"I think I need to get out of here," Violet told me finally before throwing back the last of her coffee and getting to her feet. "It's Saturday. I'm not sitting around here all day. We could go and put in some applications if you want."

"I think I need some time to get myself back together," I told her. "I'll get back to it on Monday. I promise. I just—my head is a mess right now. I need some time to think."

"Okay, well, I'm still going to go out," Violet replied. "You can still come with me if you want."

I shook my head, waving my hand. "No, you go ahead. I don't want to hold you up. I think I just need to be a grump for today."

"All right, but don't get used to it," she warned me, only half-joking. "I'm going to get you up and at it again as soon as I get the chance, okay?"

"Oh, I know," I said.

She ruffled my hair as she went through to her room to change. I wished I had the energy to get up off my ass in that moment, but honestly, I could have laid my head on the couch and fallen asleep again right there. I couldn't give into any of this for too long, but for now, I needed to mope a little. To figure out what I actually wanted.

Times like this were when I really felt the distance between me and the rest of my family. It wasn't that I didn't want to be close to them, more that I felt this space between us when I was at a loss in this way. They all seemed to have their lives together, whereas every time I got close, I found mine spinning out of control once more, the gaps that I filled emptying again far too quickly for me to patch up. When I next saw them, they were going to ask about my job, and I was going to have to admit to them it had all fallen apart and I was back to square one once more.

Or I could go back and work for him again.

He hadn't hired anyone new yet. That had to count for something, didn't it? It must have meant that he still had a little time for me at least. That he missed having me around if he couldn't find someone to fill that gap so easily. And Melanie seemed pretty set on having me back, and she knew her son better than anyone, right? She knew what he needed. And she seemed pretty determined that he needed me, no matter how much he tried to dissuade her of that notion.

Maybe it would be easier to just go back there. Sure, I'd have to do a little groveling, and sure, I would have to deal with the fact that he was seeing other women, but maybe it was for the best. I knew the job, I knew what I was doing, and it paid well—not to mention the fact that I wouldn't have to admit to my family that I had lost my job. Or why.

Shit, I knew they would have enough fun trying to guess why I had lost the job, and if they found out it had been because I was involved with the man I was working for, they would never let me live it down.

And I didn't want to push Violet any further than I already had. She had been so sweet to me this whole time, but even she was starting to get annoyed with how far I was taking this. Who could blame her? Anyone else would have booted me out onto the street a hell of a long time ago, but she had stuck by me. There was only so much patience she would have, and I didn't want to push it any further than I already had.

I couldn't just sit around on the couch all day. Leaving the house wasn't something I could manage, but there was no way that lazing around feeling sorry for myself was going to make things any better. I at least needed to shower and to put on some real clothes.

I could clean the house, too. Then at least Violet might see some reason for keeping me around. The last thing I needed was her changing her mind about keeping me around here and kicking me out the way she probably should have a long time ago.

I jumped into a quick shower, took a rest on the bed for a while, and brushed my hair and slipped into some comfortable old jeans and a faded tee. It was hardly my most glamorous look, but I didn't care. The fact that I had clothes on at all felt like something of a victory right now.

I even headed over to the bathroom and put on a little mascara, fluttering my lashes at myself in the mirror, trying to feel myself at least a little. It was a long shot, but I wanted to feel good and confident, especially if I was going to go back out and start looking for work once more. And it wasn't like I had much of a choice.

I started cleaning the house, promising myself that by the time Violet got back from wherever she was, it would be spotless, top to bottom.

Soon enough, I got into the pace of it, turning on some music and dancing around to try and shake off some of the irritation that had been hanging over my head this entire time. Okay, this was actually kind of fun.

Maybe I could get into cleaning. Scrubbing down an office after hours so that I wouldn't have to bother with any actual people. My family would hate it, but that wouldn't bother me. I knew that anything I did, they would probably find some way to pick holes in it, and frankly, at this point, I only cared about pleasing myself. I had spent far too long trying to make other people happy, but right now, that was over and done with.

"Lilah?"

I looked around and saw Violet staring at me like she had just seen a ghost. I cocked an eyebrow at her.

"What's up with you?" I asked as I turned the music down so I could hear her.

She shook her head. "I just got back."

"Oh okay?"

"And—and—" she stammered, like she was still trying to wrap her head around what had just happened.

"Is everything okay?" I asked.

She nodded, but before she could tell me what was up, I figured it out all at once.

Damian pushed into the apartment. He was sweaty as hell and looked like he had run across town to be there.

My jaw dropped as I tried to work out what the fuck he was even doing there—but before I could say a word, he spoke.

Chapter Sixteen

Damian

I KNEW I SHOULDN'T have been here. Seriously, I knew I should have known better than to give in to the feelings that had driven me down here, but now I was standing there in her apartment staring at her, and I knew I had to come out with something.

"We need to talk," I told her, and I glanced around at Violet, who had been the one to open the door and let me in.

She held up her hands and stepped right out once more, not bothering to hang around to see what was going to happen. Probably for the best. I didn't know what was going to go down while I was here, and I didn't want an audience for it.

"You can't just turn up here," Lilah shot back at me, crossing her arms over her chest and eyeing me with open disdain.

"Well, looks like I'm here anyway," I told her. "So are you going to talk to me?"

"What do you want to talk about?" she asked.

I didn't even know. I hadn't thought that far ahead. Truth be told, I had just been at that driving range, trying to blow off some of the steam my father had sent coursing through me, and it hadn't worked, and this was the only place I could think of to come where I could do that.

I missed her. I had missed her at the range more than I had missed her anywhere else before. Because when she had gone to the range with me, everything had felt a little lighter. Everything had felt like it didn't matter as much as I was letting it matter. It reminded me of our trip to California, when everything had been going so right up until the moment where it all fell apart for good and I was left trying to put the pieces together.

Still, I had no idea what I even intended to say to her, but I had to get it out and say it to her face before I lost my mind. Everything else felt out of my control lately. At the very least, I could get this back under control for a little while.

"What the hell was that in the coffee shop?" I demanded finally, remembering the last time we had seen one another.

She looked away from me, her eyes lowering. "I didn't want to see you with some other woman."

I could have corrected her and told her that Tamsin was nothing to me and that my father had just tried dangling her in front of me because he thought I was the same brand of pathetic that he was, but I doubted she would have believed me.

"What difference does it make to you?" I asked. "Because you were the one who ended it. What does it matter if I was dating the whole of New York City?"

"Because I thought we had something," she exploded back at me. The pain in her voice was clear, even to me, and I was a little surprised to hear the passion with which she spoke. As though she could hardly believe that she had to have this conversation, could hardly believe that I hadn't put the pieces together myself yet.

"Then why did you end it?" I fired back, exasperated. "If we had something? If you really thought that, you wouldn't—"

"I wouldn't have ended things?" she asked. "After the way you treated me, I couldn't put up with that, Damian. You know that. I don't want to be spoken to like that. I don't want to be treated like I'm just some—like I'm just some accessory to your life."

Okay, that took me off guard. Of everything I had expected her to say, that was the last thing. Was that really how she felt? Had I really been that shitty to her? I'd never been with someone long enough to hear what they really felt about me, but she was laying it out for me now, and there was no denying the pain that was written all over her face as she stood there before me, staring at me like she was pleading with me to understand what was going through her mind.

"It's not fair," she continued. "You were so romantic, and you were acting like there was actually something real between us. And then I wake up that morning and it's all just changed."

"It was work," I said.

She shook her head. "There's always going to be an excuse to treat the people around you like shit if you're looking hard enough," she replied, a deep sadness in her voice. "But most people don't go looking for it. Most people don't want to find it. You do. You did."

I didn't know what to say to her for a moment. My blood felt like it was boiling inside my veins. Maybe she was right. Maybe I didn't take as well to being talked to like that as anyone else in the world did. But how could I be expected to? How could I be expected to just detach from work when that had been everything in my life for so long? She had come into my life as part of that, for goodness sake. She couldn't seriously think I was just going to forget about it.

"You don't understand how it is with me and my work," I snapped back, my voice tenser than it had to be.

She understood me in a way that nobody else did, and I wasn't sure I liked that. Sometimes when I was around her, I could feel my skin crawling, could feel that deep sense of being known by someone else that I hadn't had in so long—being known for better and for worse, being seen even in the ways that I wanted to hide.

"I do," she told me. "I worked for you, remember? And you're moving pretty quick to replace me. You don't get to tell me that I don't understand it. I understand it better than anyone else in your life right now. Even whatever new assistant you hire to take my place."

"You're the one who quit, remember?" I reminded her hotly. "You didn't expect me to just sit around waiting for someone to come in and take your place, did you?"

"No, but I didn't think you would move so quickly," she said. "Not with that. Not with—all of it."

Her voice was tinged with hurt, but she was papering over those cracks with defensiveness, her attitude meant to throw me off and remind me that I was nothing more than a regret to her. It was something I did too, but having it tossed in my direction, it was a hard thing to wrap my head around.

"I'm sorry that I didn't spend longer mourning over what we had, but I'm not in the habit of hanging around and waiting for someone else to catch up with me when they were the ones to call it quits in the first place," I told her.

I could see the reaction, the pain crossing over her face, but I ignored it. I wanted that. Maybe that was what I needed right now, to know she hurt as much as I did. She had walked away from me, and there was some part of me, no matter how childish, that wanted to show her that I could just walk away from her too.

"Good, because I've moved on too," she snapped back at me, crossing her arms tightly over her chest and glaring at me. "So I don't think we have much more to say to each other, do you?"

"I guess not," I replied, and there was a beat of silence between us.

Even when she was angry, the way her eyes blazed into mine was enough to get my blood running a little hotter than it had been before. I didn't know what it was, but being this close to her again was making it hard for me to think straight. I didn't know what I had intended when I had come over here in the first place, but I was starting to think it might not have been as pure as I had initially imagined.

"So that's it then, and there is nothing left to talk about," she finished up. There was a finality to the way she said it. It left no room for argument, but I didn't care.

I wanted her to get mad at me. I wanted her to tell me off. I wanted her to do anything she wanted to me because that meant things didn't have to be over between us quite yet, and that was all I cared about. I wasn't ready to leave. And I knew she didn't want me to get out of there quite yet either.

"Guess not."

"So what are you still doing here?" she asked. Her arms dropped to her sides as though she was opening an invitation. Her hair was damp, her skin still glistening as though she had gotten out of a shower not long before I had arrived. The thought of the water coursing over her perfect body was enough to set a fire burning in my guts, a fire I couldn't stop or hold in any longer.

I didn't know who made the first move, and I wasn't sure it mattered much either. All I cared about was the way our mouths connected like it was what they had been waiting for since the moment I had walked through the door. I pushed her back against the wall, and she wound her arms around me and pushed her tongue deep into my mouth, letting out this helpless little moan as she did so.

Fuck, she still knew how to turn me on. I pressed my cock against her hip, letting her feel it against her thigh, letting it tell her everything that I was too stupid to say.

This was what I had come here for. I hadn't wanted to admit it when I walked through the door, but there was no doubt in my mind that this was why I was here. I needed her.

I needed the release only she could give me. Her touch, the way she held me, the way she kissed me, like she couldn't get enough—nothing else would satisfy that need that burned deep down inside of me for this woman, and I knew that. I knew there was no hiding from what I felt for her, even though I also knew we sort of hated each other right now.

"Bedroom," she breathed in my ear. "Right now. I don't want anyone else to know this is happening."

So it *was* happening then. I hadn't misread that part of it. I kissed her harder, for a moment ignoring what she had just said, having way too much fun. But I allowed her to drag me through to the bedroom, closing the door behind us as we went. And just like that, it was as though the two of us had never been apart.

Chapter Seventeen

Lilah

AS WE KISSED, I COULDN'T think about anything but what a crazy-bad idea this was.

I should have kicked him out already. I shouldn't have even let him set foot in the apartment. But there was something about the intensity of what we had, the power of what we shared, that made it impossible for me to think about anything else.

All I wanted was him. Nothing else would come close to satisfying me. And right now, that was all I gave a damn about.

I pulled him back onto the bed, and he pushed my arms above my head. I whipped them out of his grasp, knowing this was just his way of trying to control me after all I had said to him. Well, he wasn't going to get me under his thumb again that easily.

I rolled on top of him, planting my hands on his chest, feeling the hardness of his cock as it throbbed against my pussy through my jeans.

"Fuck," he growled, and he ran his hands down my sides.

I knew how he felt. It was as though everything the two of us had been trying to contain was spilling out all of a sudden, unable to hold in the way we had been trying to do for so long.

His touch, the way he held me, the way he looked at me, the way he kissed me—I didn't know how I had been able to hold off on having him for so long. Had I really thought there would be a point in time where I would never sleep with him again? I must have been crazy. Right now, everything had narrowed to this moment, to the way it made me feel when I was with him.

I reached down and unzipped his pants, sliding my hand beneath them so that I could feel his gorgeous cock in my fingers once more. He groaned, and I looked down to see his hardness swelling at my touch. I still had this power over him. I grinned, leaned down, and planted a kiss on his chin, and he grabbed me and pushed his tongue into my mouth.

Reaching over to my bedside cabinet, I found a condom and tore it open frantically before I rolled it down over his cock. He was already pulling off my pants and underwear, the two of us so starved for one another that there was no room for anything like pacing ourselves. I didn't know when Violet would come back, and frankly, the last thing I needed was for her to cast judgement on what the two of us were up to. She would have some choice words for me if she caught wind of what I was doing.

As soon as I had the condom rolled down over his cock, I kicked off my pants and lowered myself down on top of him. I let out a deep, throaty groan as I felt him push inside of me. How was it that I could already be so wet for him when we had mostly been arguing since he had walked into my apartment? Maybe it was enough just being around him really—enough to just feel that rush of passion, of power, of need that came from being close to him.

He grasped my hips and pushed me as far down onto his cock as I could go, greedy for the sensation of me taking every inch of him. I cried out, and he grasped my face in his hands and kissed me again. He was so rough, using me any way he saw fit. Frankly, the passion with which he was taking me was just getting me closer and closer to the edge.

He sat up, wrapped his arms around me, and started to thrust into me hard. My whole body was shaking as I tried to keep up with the intensity of his movements inside of me, and I loved every moment of it. Ever since I had last seen him, I felt as though I had been overthinking everything, but now, all of it just came down to how much I wanted him, and nothing else mattered. It was a relief to give into something so basic.

I kissed him again as he drove himself deep inside of me, filling me up over and over again with his full length. He let out these deep, growling groans every time he moved within me. I knew he wanted me, knew he needed me, knew that everything in him was waiting for this moment the same way I had been waiting for it, even if I hadn't known it when he had walked through the door.

I pushed my hand between us so I could play with my clit as he fucked me, so close now that I needed to go over the edge and come before I lost my damn mind. He slowed, moving in circles, really grinding himself as deep as he could go, and I gasped as I felt myself finally give in and tip over the edge and into my release.

When I came, it didn't take long for him to follow. I felt his cock twitch, and the satisfying sensation of him finishing inside of me began. He pressed a kiss to my collarbone before he eased himself out of me and planted me down on the bed beside him.

Now that it was over, I had no choice but to actually talk to him.

I had no idea what it was I wanted to say, but there was so much running through my head that I didn't know where to start. Did I bring up the other girl I had seen him with? Did I mention the fact that his very own mother had been trying to get me to come back and work for him? Did he know that? Had he been the one to send her out there? I had no idea and no clue how I was meant to go about getting that all out of him either.

He looked over at me as he slipped off the condom and disposed of it. I felt a little flush of nerves, not sure what I was meant to say to him now that we'd gotten that part out of the way.

"Hope you didn't just cheat with me," I blurted out finally. It was hardly the coolest thing I could have said, but it was relevant at least.

I didn't want to be getting in the way of someone else's relationship. And better that I started there rather than bringing up his mother when he had only just pulled himself out of me. Things might have been awkward between us, but I didn't want to make them quite that awkward if I could avoid it.

"I didn't," he replied.

I cocked my head at him. I remembered the smile he had given that girl at the coffee shop when he had seen her for the first time, and I wasn't sure I believed it.

"Okay, but would that girl you were with at the coffee shop be very happy about this if she knew about it?" I asked.

He shook his head again. This time, he looked a little irritated that he had to put me right.

"I'm not with her," he replied bluntly.

I furrowed my brow. "Yeah, but you'd have to say that."

"No, seriously," he said. "I'm not with her. That's just some girl my dad sent along to try and convince me to go along with the bullshit he's pulling this week."

"You're serious?" I asked.

He nodded. "I'm not seeing anyone. I'm too busy trying to make sure my dad doesn't tank my business."

He eyed me for a moment, and a small smile flicked up his lips. He seemed amused at how intense my reaction had been. I supposed I deserved that.

"Good to know you're still jealous, though," he teased me lightly.

I parted my lips with every intention of protesting, but then he spoke again.

"Trust me," he said. "I haven't had time for anything but work. My dad has been making a mess of things. Though I'm sure he's trying to pretend that he isn't right now. He actually sent that girl out to meet with me, to try and get me on board for a deal he wants to make."

"Shit, that's crazy," I muttered. "He really thought he could just send a girl out there and you would go along with anything that he suggested?"

"Yeah, he really did," he replied.

I couldn't imagine how unlucky that girl who'd had to deal with him must have felt. I knew him pretty well by now, well enough that I could guess just how well that had gone. Even though I knew I shouldn't have found it funny, I had to admit it was hard to keep in the little flicker of amusement at the back of my mind.

"It's ridiculous, but I guess he thinks it would work on him, so it must work on everyone around him too."

"He really doesn't know you at all, huh?" I said.

He shook his head. "Not one little bit," he replied, and he suddenly sounded a little sad, as though he couldn't believe he had to deal with all of this.

I wanted to take his hand and comfort him, but I didn't know if we were there yet. A few minutes before, we had been arguing. Just because we had punctuated that with some seriously good sex didn't mean that either of us had forgotten what had come before.

"What are you going to do about him?" I asked.

He shook his head. "I don't know. I've been trying to do damage control since we—since I got back to the city, but there's only so much I can do when he won't slow down or stop with any of this."

"That's bullshit," I said. I didn't have any right to be commentating on what was going on with his life, but I was too angry to be quiet.

His father was a failure, at least when it came to business. He was being shady invoking his son's name to try and pick up the pieces that he had left behind. Seriously, this was a whole new level of parental interference—and I had thought that Melanie was bad enough for it.

Before I could say another word, though, I heard the door to the apartment open and my stomach dropped as I realized Violet must have been back already. Probably curious to see if I had gotten rid of him yet, to find out the gossip of what he had been here for in the first place.

If she saw him leaving my room—oh shit.

"Get dressed!" I hissed to him. "I don't want Violet to see you in here."

He scrambled to grab his clothes, and I peeked around the door. Violet was already coming toward it, and I bounded out and closed it behind me.

"Is he gone already?" she asked.

I nodded. "Oh, yeah, he's gone. He didn't want to stick around long. I threw him out."

I prayed he wasn't making too much noise in there. I could see some doubt on Violet's face, but she wasn't calling me on it. I didn't want to have to explain to my best friend why the hell I had the man I told her I hated in my bedroom.

"Could you check if we need toilet paper?" I blurted out to her. It was the only thing I could think of that would give me the space to smuggle him out of there before she caught on.

She furrowed her brow at me. "Why can't you check?"

"Would you mind?" I suggested, hustling her toward the bathroom. "I'm going to go out and grab some stuff. I just want to know if I need to get any of that, too."

I managed to close the door behind her, and I waved my hand wildly toward Damian to coax him out of my bedroom. I didn't care whether he was dressed or not. He was going to have to get the hell out of there. Otherwise, there was going to be trouble.

I managed to shove him in the direction of the door and close it behind him just as Violet stuck her head out of the bathroom once more.

"I guess we could use some more if you're going out," she replied. "Did you just open the door?"

"No, no. It must have been your mind playing tricks on you."

She stared at me for a moment, waiting for me to crack, but I just looked back at her and hoped I was actually selling this right now.

"Right," she said, but I could tell that she didn't buy any of it. "So you going to tell me what Damian was doing here? Or is that still totally a secret?"

"I think I could spill the beans," I replied, and I wracked my brain to come up with what I could tell her that wouldn't blow our cover.

Because the last thing I needed right now was for someone else to know about what had happened between us. I didn't even understand how I felt about it yet.

Chapter Eighteen

Damian

"SO I'VE BEEN LOOKING over the assets of the company, and it seems like moving in for a takeover is going to be easier than we thought," Karen, my attorney, told me as I sat opposite her in her office.

"Tell me exactly what you think we'll need to do," I replied.

She nodded at once. She was taking this as seriously as I was, and I was damn glad to have someone on my side who seemed to make everything a little easier and less confusing.

Ever since I had gone to Lilah's place a few days before, I hadn't been able to stop thinking about her. Half of me wanted to walk straight back down there, pull her into my arms again, and tell her to forget about that new job or that new life because she was coming back to me. And the other half of me knew there was nothing to gain from getting hung up on her, and I should have been smart enough to move on by now. And yet...

It had all started because of that meeting with my father. That meeting where he had tried to fight with me about what he thought was best for the company. Well, if he wasn't going to listen to me, I was going to have to move in and do what I had been planning for a long time now. A hostile takeover.

It wasn't exactly ideal, but he hadn't given me much of a choice. If we could have worked together on this, I would have jumped at the chance, but if he was going to keep dragging my name into his business, then the least I could do was make sure I wanted to be associated with it.

That was what Karen and I were going over this afternoon, everything we would need to put together to make sure nobody could catch us out as we tried to make the move to take over his business. Everything would have to be perfectly in place. The last thing I needed was to make the choice to take him over and then have it fall apart on me.

He would push back against it, but I knew it was for the best. I could take it from him, pull it apart, and put it back together in a way that worked. Hell, when I was done, I could even put him back in charge of it if he wanted—if he had proved himself by then. I just didn't want him dragging the family name through the mud anymore, and I sure as hell wasn't going to just sit back and let it happen.

Not to mention I felt like I needed to take something into my control right now. I had been spending enough time feeling out of it lately, feeling like everything was coming apart, and this was the only thing I could think of I could challenge.

My father wasn't going to be happy about it—not at first—but when he got past his pride, he would see this was the best thing for both of us. I could get his company back on the straight and narrow again, and he could step back and go do whatever it was he liked to do with all those girls who he couldn't seem to get enough of.

"And how long do you think it's going to be before we can make the move?" I asked Karen.

She shook her head. "I couldn't say right now, but I would say at some point in the next month. I would advise that you keep this as much to yourself as possible. Don't let anyone else in on it unless they have to know. If someone at the company finds out, they could shift things around, and that would mean we'd have to come up with a different approach."

"Of course," I said, nodding. "I'll keep this under wraps as much as possible. The last thing I want is for my father to find out about it."

"Exactly," she said, and she checked her watch. "I think that's all I have to share for today. Can we put another meeting on the books for later in the week? I want to keep moving on this as much as we can. We need the momentum to get where we want to go."

"Yeah, of course," I replied.

Soon enough, we had set another time and place to meet, and I was out of there and headed back to my own office. And even though at least a little of the mess in my head was starting to clear, some of it was just getting worse.

I needed to see Lilah again. It was that simple. There wasn't a question of *if*. There was just a question of *when*. Ever since we had seen each other last, I had been starving for her, unable to get her out of my head. She had kicked me out of her apartment pretty fucking quickly, and I got the feeling the people in her life wouldn't have been too happy if I came back into it, but maybe it could be different this time. Maybe.

Or maybe I needed to work on myself before I got to that point with her. I didn't want to bring her back into my life, only to let her down again the way I had before. I didn't know what I had done wrong, but I didn't want to do that to her again. I had hurt her, and there was no way in hell I was going to let that go down again. Not after she had made so much effort and put in so much time with me. Not after she had tried so hard.

When I got back to my office, I couldn't help but pause for a moment and look at the empty desk she used to occupy right outside my office. I could have hired someone else to take that position by now, but I was still hoping she would come back. I didn't want anyone else there because there was only one person who came close to doing the job the way I wanted.

I stepped into my office, and of course, my mother was in there waiting for me.

"There you are!" she exclaimed. "I thought you were never going to get back."

"What are you doing here?" I asked, already tired by the thought of the conversation that lay ahead of me.

What did she want now? I was sure I was going to fail on giving it to her, just the way I had been all this time.

"I just wanted to come by and see you," she replied, her eyes fixed to mine. "Because it seems like you've been having a hard time lately."

That caught me off guard. I knew she always meant the best for me, but sometimes, it felt as though she could forget that as much as anyone else could. She was so busy sticking her nose into my life that I was surprised by the revelation she actually cared enough to ask.

"I'm fine," I replied.

She crossed her arms over her chest and looked at me. "Take a seat." She nodded toward the spot I usually did all my work from. "I think we need to talk."

"About what?"

"I'm not sure, but something's bothering you," she replied pointedly. "You want to talk about it?"

Some part of me wanted to tell her I had work to do and I was too busy to sit around talking about my feelings all day. But maybe that was my problem in the first place. Maybe I needed to detach from this idea of doing things right, of making sure that everything ran just the way I wanted it to. Maybe I should have been a little more open. Maybe that was what Lilah had been asking for from me all this time.

"It's a lot of stuff really," I said finally, and she gestured for me to keep going. So I did.

There was so much stuff I didn't even realize I had been holding on to, and it all came spilling out of me before I could stop it. There was so much I had wanted to tell someone, but I hadn't been able to find anyone to share it all with.

I told her about Lilah. I told her I wanted her back, even though I didn't go into the specific details of just why that might have been. I even told her about Dad and everything that had been happening with the business, and though I could tell she wanted nothing more than to trash talk him, she let me just spill it all to her instead.

When I was done, it felt like a weight had lifted from my shoulders. I hadn't known how badly I needed to talk to someone about all of this, but it suddenly felt like I should have known that all along. I needed a therapist. Shit, I needed several therapists probably, given all the shit that was going on in my head at any given time.

Sometimes, it felt like there was so much shit crammed up inside there that I couldn't keep any of it straight. I needed something to shake it loose, something that would just kick me out of the funk I found myself in.

"That sounds like a lot to deal with," Mom murmured when I was all done.

I shook my head. "Not really," I replied.

I didn't know why I felt the need to brush her off like that, but something about accepting that this really was as much as I thought it was would have been too much for me to handle.

"Yeah, it is," she corrected me gently. "I'm your mom. I know better than you with all of this, remember?"

I managed to smile at her. I knew she meant well, even if there were times when I wanted nothing more than to lock the doors and keep her out of my life for a while.

"I remember," I said. "And thanks. For listening, I mean. I know it's all a mess."

"It'll figure itself out," she told me.

From anyone else, I would have brushed that off as nothing more than a platitude, a promise that they could in no way be sure they would follow through on. But from her, it was harder to brush off. Maybe I even believed it somewhere at the back of my mind. Maybe I even thought she was telling the truth.

"Yeah," I said. "It will."

For that moment at least, I could believe it. I had no idea how in the hell it was going to figure itself out, but I had no choice but to believe that it would. The other possibility was just too much for me to take.

And maybe a little optimism was what I needed in my life.

Chapter Nineteen

Lilah

I PACED DOWN THE STREET, trying to keep myself from letting my nerves get the better of me, but how the hell was I meant to do that when it felt like my brain was going to burst?

I couldn't stop thinking about what had happened between Damian and me. I missed him like crazy, even though we'd only had sex once when he had come to my place.

I wanted to talk to him again but I didn't know how I was meant to do that. If I left it much longer, the two of us would get to that point where it was way too awkward to spend time together. I needed to do something to make sure I didn't let it go that far.

But I was meant to be out there looking for another job. I had no clue what I was looking for exactly, but I would take anything I could right now. My brain was too stuffed full of shit to really focus on what mattered, but maybe that was okay. Maybe that was what I needed to work through to come out the other side and feel a little saner.

Maybe, maybe, maybe.

I had turned in a few resumes that day, but I wasn't sure any of the companies were going to get back to me. One of them had noticed I had worked for Damian, and they'd seemed pretty amused by the revelation.

"You know the company?" I'd asked.

The man had nodded. "Yeah, we used to work together," he replied. I scanned his voice for any kind of weight to those words, but I couldn't find any. What was that supposed to mean? I had no idea, but I would take it as good news for the time being.

"That's great," I replied smoothly, playing it to my advantage. "Then you know just what I'm qualified for then."

"I suppose I do," the man, a little older than me, replied, and I wondered if his mind was going to the same place that mine was—that what I was qualified for was sliding into bed with my boss.

I hoped news of what I had been getting up to with Damian hadn't gone anywhere, but it was hard to know that when I couldn't ask outright.

I was wandering through the city now, trying to find anywhere that had a vacancy sign in the window so that I could hand in my resume and make sure I didn't let Vi down any more than I already had. She had stuck by me through all of this, and I was out here for her, to make sure she didn't have to do that again for the length of our friendship. From this point onward, I was going to make sure I was the one who could cover her if she needed it. I didn't want her to feel like I was letting her down. Not once. Not ever again. I had already asked for enough from her, and that ended right here, right now.

But with my head full of Damian, it was hard to make a dent in the stack of resumes that I had printed out. I hadn't spoken to anyone about what had happened between us, not yet, especially not Violet, who I'd wanted to keep at arm's length as best I could. I just wanted to keep it to myself so that nobody could judge me for it. I knew that hooking up with him again had been a mistake, but that didn't mean I needed the whole world to point that out for me.

Sigh. I had to get back home before it got dark out, and I was tempted to get myself a drink or three. Maybe that would help clear up some of the doubt at the edge of my mind.

I turned to start the long walk home, and with every step I took, I found myself more certain I was going to tell my roommate about what had happened. I wasn't going to be able to get through this if I didn't have her on my side.

By the time I got back home, my mind was made up. I was going to talk to her about all of it. She would be able to point me in the right direction. And I frigging needed someone to do that for me right now.

When I came through the door, I found her sitting on the couch, arranging some delicate pink tissue paper over the top of another thicker card.

"What are you up to?" I asked.

She glanced up at me and shrugged. "Oh, I just thought I would get going on some of the baby-shower invitations."

"Even though we don't have a guestlist," I teased.

She cocked her eyebrow at me. "Or a theme, or a venue, or anything else. But yeah, I thought it would be fun. And they look pretty cute, don't you think?"

"They really do," I said as I sat down next to her on the couch. I took a deep breath, trying to get myself ready for what I needed to tell her.

"Violet, there's something I want to talk to you about," I announced.

She looked at me with a furrow in her brow. "Oh, shit, what's going on?" She sounded a little exhausted by the very thought of what I might be about to come out with. I didn't blame her. These last few weeks had just been full-blown chaos, and she was probably expecting me to announce a surprise baby or something like that.

"Nothing's going on," I assured her. "It's just stuff that's already happened. That's all. I could use some advice on it."

"Hit me," she replied, leaning back in her seat and locking her fingers behind her head.

I filled her in on all of it—on the sex with Damian, on the new jobs I'd applied for, on moving on and feeling like I still had that tie to him. On running into him at the coffee shop and seeing him with that other woman, even though he denied anything was going on with her. I wasn't sure if I believed him quite yet, but maybe I would start to come around to it.

"Shit, that's a lot," she said, shaking her head and running her hand through her hair. "You really applied for a job at a place that used to work with him?"

"Yeah, why?"

"Well, do you think you might be doing it just to spite him?"

I furrowed my brow and shook my head at once. "Oh, no, nothing like that," I replied quickly. "It's just that they were there. I didn't know they used to work with him."

"You think that the breakup was amicable?"

"It's not like they were dating," I pointed out.

She shrugged. "Yeah, but do you think that you going to work there would piss him off?"

I parted my lips to protest, but honestly, I hadn't even thought that far ahead. Maybe she had a point.

"I don't know," I admitted. "It's not really where my head's at right now, to be honest. I'm just trying to stay focused on actually getting back to work. If it upsets him, then I guess it upsets him. There's not much I can do about that."

"Hmm, I guess," she said. "But if he was to get upset by it, how would you feel? Do you think it would make you want to quit?"

"I don't think so," I replied, and then, more firmly, I corrected my-self. "No. No, I'm not going to let that stop me. I don't know what's happening with us. I don't want to keep letting him get in the way of moving forward, you know?"

"I totally agree with that," she said. "You need to do what's right for you and you can't let any guy tell you what that looks like."

"No. Otherwise, you'll be making invitations for my baby shower before we've even managed to get my sister's out of the way."

She laughed and shook her head.

"Yeah, I don't think we're quite there yet," I replied, and I cringed at the thought.

That was just what I needed on top of everything else—the chaos of getting pregnant. Shit, talk about a nightmare. Just thinking about it was enough to make my skin crawl.

"Glad to hear it," she replied. "But make sure you're being safe next time you have some crazy hookup, all right?"

"You sound like my mom." I laughed.

She wagged her finger at me playfully. "I'm just saying, no getting pregnant on my watch. I love you but housing an unemployed single mother—that might be pushing me a little too far in the roommate department."

"In that case, I'll just make sure I don't tell you," I joked.

She grinned and squeezed my hand. "You know if something like that did happen, you could tell me about it. I know I'm not exactly the most maternal person, but if you needed help or anything, I'd want you to be able to come to me to get it."

"You're honestly the sweetest," I told her. "And I don't think you're right about not being maternal. You look out for me, don't you?"

"Yeah, but that's only because sometimes it feels like you're not looking out for yourself," she teased.

I rolled my eyes at her playfully. "So what you're saying is that just because I slept with the same guy I said I want nothing more to do with, I can't be trusted? I don't know where you're getting that idea."

"You want something to drink?" she asked.

"Just a coffee for me," I replied. "Thanks. You want to get down to some of this planning for the baby shower? I suppose I should actually start taking it seriously."

"Ya think?" she said brightly.

I sat back in my seat and stared off into space for a moment, reflecting on the conversation we'd just had. It was hard for me to believe all of this was really happening.

I had been with him again, and it felt like it had set off this stream of fire that tore through my whole life. I wanted to be near him, but at the same time, I knew I had to give myself the time and space to do everything I needed to move on to something that didn't involve him. To a life that didn't revolve around Damian.

But I wasn't sure I was ready for that yet. Not when he was so fresh in my memory. Not when he was all I could think about. Not when it seemed as though every inch of my body was crying out for him once more.

I thought of him, all the way across the city, and hoped against hope he was thinking of me too.

That I wasn't alone in this burning need.

Chapter Twenty

Damian

"OH, HEY!"

I heard a familiar voice and looked up from my phone, already a little annoyed that someone had distracted me from work.

I was out on my break from the office, the time I forced myself to take off so that I didn't go totally crazy all cooped up in there, but that didn't mean I couldn't keep checking my emails when I was out. But when I saw who it was who had greeted me, I stopped in my tracks.

"Oh, hi, Violet," I said.

Lilah's roommate. Okay, she had been the last person I'd expected to run into down here, heading for lunch in the business district, but here she was, standing right in front of me with a coffee in her hand and a smile on her face.

"I didn't expect to see you out of your office," she said brightly. "Thought you were chained to that desk by the sounds of it."

"Yeah, well, got to get out once in a while, or I'll go crazy," I said carefully. I didn't know how much she might have known about what was going on between her roommate and me, and frankly, I didn't want to be the one to expose anything.

"Right," she said. "By the way, you left your jacket at our place. Thought you might want to pick it up at some point."

My lips parted in surprise. She'd known I'd been there, of course, since she had been the one to let me in. But I had no idea if Lilah had told her more than that.

What did she know?

Her voice was a little cool, as though she was testing the waters and seeing just how much she could get away with. I didn't want to give her anything more than I needed to, and I did everything I could to keep my tone as casual as I could. No need to feed into anything else she was putting out there.

"Yeah, I'll stop by when I get the chance and pick it up," I said.

"Appreciate it," she said. "I don't think Lilah does too well with the reminders of you hanging around."

"Then she could always call me and ask me to pick it up herself," I shot back, a little tense. I didn't appreciate being spoken to this way, and I didn't know why I was getting the third fucking degree when I had just walked out of my office.

Violet had seemed pretty chill the last time I had seen her, and I didn't know what it was that had changed to make her so snarky to me.

"Yeah, if she's not too busy," she replied.

I knew I shouldn't rise to take the bait, but I couldn't resist. "Busy with what?"

"Her new job," she replied casually. "Teller and Evans? I'm sure you've heard of them."

I tensed up, knowing she was just trying to goad me. There was no way Lilah could already be working a new job at that place.

I had partnered with them before, and we just weren't able to make it work. Things were a little cool between us, but the chances of Lilah knowing a thing about that seemed slim, unless she had actually met with them. It was possible, I guessed, that they knew Lilah had worked for me and wanted to make a point to use that against me, but what kind of chance was there of that?

It seemed like a long way to go just to make sure they got one over on someone they used to work with. I tried not to think about it, but I could tell Violet had read into some of the discomfort in my head.

"Glad to hear she's back at work," I replied coolly. "Let her know that I send my congratulations, all right?"

"Sure, but wouldn't you rather pass it on yourself?" she asked. "Since you seem like such a regular around the house these days."

"Maybe I will," I said. "When I come around to pick up my coat."

"Yeah, sure you will," she answered me, defiant. "If you're not trying to avoid her, huh?"

"She's going to be busy with her new job," I said. "Not like there's much that I could do to get in her way now."

"She's only there because you fired her," Violet said.

I shook my head. Okay, now I was getting pissed. This was meant to be time for myself, and yet, she was coming at me like I had done something wrong.

"She's the one who left the job, in case you forgot about it," I snapped. "Sounds like she doesn't have anything to be worried about, though, given that she's starting work again so soon."

"I bet you'd prefer it if she came crawling back to you, huh?" she asked, narrowing her eyes in my direction.

"I don't care where she's crawling to," I replied. "Not my business, not my concern. That clear?"

"Yeah, it sure isn't," she fired back, and then it seemed as though some of the tension in her body started to ease out a little. Her head drooped down to her chest, and she let out a long sigh, as though she didn't even really want to be having this conversation with me.

"I'm sorry," she muttered. "It's just—it's hard, you know? I've seen how much of an impact all of this has had on her, and I just want someone to blame for it."

"I get that," I replied. "But I have places to be. And I'm not the one at fault for any of this. If you speak to her about what happened, you'll figure that out soon enough."

"What makes you think I haven't?" she asked.

I was confused. Why was she coming at me like this if she already knew what had happened between Lilah and me? It didn't make much sense to me, but I got the feeling she didn't care. This was a woman being protective of her friend above all else, and there wasn't going to be much in the way of reasoning with her.

"I think I should get back to work," I told her firmly, making sure I gave her no space to come back at me with something smart.

"Sure you do," she replied, eyeing me for a moment. "I guess without Lilah there, you have more to take care of, don't you?"

"Suppose so," I replied. "Send her my best regards about her new job. I'm sure she'll do well there."

"I'm sure she will too," she said, and with that, she brushed past me and walked off down the street, on with her day. Probably not going to think about me for another second. But I wasn't going to be so lucky.

Was Lilah really going to work with those guys? It made sense, given that they covered some of the same territory as I did and she had her experience working with me. But would they have signed her up so quickly? Contracts in, already at the office, already making the place her own?

Maybe they knew she had worked for me, and they wanted to make a point of proving they could get anything they wanted, even if it meant taking the woman who used to work for me.

I felt a creeping dread crawling down my spine. Was that *why* they had hired her? Because she had worked with me? Because they knew she would have something down and dirty on me and because they hoped she was willing to come out with everything she had picked up from working alongside me?

She had known pretty much every inch of the office, of the work we had done together, Maybe that was what they had wanted from her in the first place.

I didn't like this. I didn't like it one little bit.

I turned on my heel and stormed back to the office. I was sure I was just letting my nerves get the better of me, but who could blame me? Things between Lilah and me were complicated, and I had no idea what she might have done to get back at me.

I felt like the two of us were starting to move past working together, like maybe we were getting to something else that actually worked for us. But if I made a mess of this, all of that would be over again.

What if I had stayed? Asked her not to push me out the door? Asked if we could just talk this out for a while? Maybe I wouldn't have anything to worry about. But as it was, I was nervous.

I knew she had it out for me. The two of us had tripped over each other, trying to make sense of everything we had been through together, and now we were so wrapped up in our pasts that I didn't know if we could move forward.

I remembered what I had said to my mother about her—how I missed her, how I wished I could have her back. Even if that was just for work, I meant it. My life felt emptier without her in it. Slower. Like everything had taken a step back and was waiting for me to catch up.

Now she had started working somewhere else, and I had no damn right to claim her for myself any longer.

Did she know how much I missed her? I wished I could beam it right into her head. Well, I had to pick up that jacket. Maybe I could make a point of seeing her then, showing her that I was still thinking about her even though things between us were over.

But were they? If they were truly done, there would have been no reason for her roommate to come out swinging at me like that. She had been protective, but protective over what? I had no idea.

Because I wasn't trying to mess up Lilah's life. Though she might have been trying to do that to me—and I would need to keep my head in the game to make sure I wasn't being fucked over by the very woman I had almost convinced myself I loved when we had been traveling together.

Shit. It felt like all I had at every turn was more enemies everywhere I looked. What was I doing to push the people closest to me away? It didn't make sense. It wasn't fair. I just wished I could go back in time and find some way to undo the mistakes that had led me to this point.

My father was using my name and seemed to want nothing more to do with me than that, and Lilah, the first woman I had let into my life in years, was pushing back against the thought of even seeing me again. Something didn't add up. And I got the feeling that it was me.

As I walked down the busy street, I couldn't help but feel the weight of my own loneliness bearing down on my shoulders. Maybe I had been the problem all along.

And maybe I needed to do something to fix that.

Chapter Twenty-One

Lilah

"GET UP," VIOLET CALLED to me as she marched into my bedroom and started sorting through my clothes. "You've got an interview."

I lifted my head from my pillow, furrowing my brow at her in total confusion. "Sorry, what?" I mumbled, propping myself up on my elbow and trying to work out what they hell she was going on about.

"With that Teller company," she replied. "I called up to follow up on the resume, and they said they have space for an interview later today. You have to get up so you can get down there in time."

"Why did you do that?" I asked, utterly and totally confused. I knew she wanted the best for me, but surely even for her, this was overstepping the line.

"Because I think they would be a really good place for you to work," she replied, but it was more than that. She had been pretty hands-off most of this time so far, trying to keep her nose out of my business, but something had clearly shifted.

"What's happening?" I asked again.

She tossed some clothes in my direction. "Here, I think these would be good for today," she told me, not bothering to answer my question.

I cocked an eyebrow at her. I had some serious questions, and I got the feeling I wasn't going to get an answer to a single one of them.

"Fine, fine," I said, rolling out of bed and pinning the covers to myself so that I didn't flash her a boob by accident. "Can you give me a second to clean myself up? I need to look up the address and everything."

"I've got everything taken care of for you. You just need to get out of bed and go." She checked her watch. "Preferably in the next fifteen minutes."

"Damn, Vi, you couldn't have given me a little more time to get my shit together?" I asked.

She shook her head. "Because then you might have had the time to talk yourself out of it," she pointed out, flashing me a smile. "I thought it was for the best that you just get up and go."

"Yeah, well, in the future, I'll be the judge of that," I muttered, but I was grateful she had gone to all this effort to make something good happen for me.

I got dressed and gave myself a pep talk in the mirror. I could do this. If I could get a job with Damian, then I could get a job with this guy. What was it I had done to land that position again? Oh, yeah, I had insulted him when I thought he was someone else.

Maybe that approach wasn't exactly foolproof. Anyway, I could make this work. Violet had gone to all this effort for me, and I wasn't going to let her down. Not a chance in hell.

I rolled out of the door just in time to make it down there, and sure enough, as soon as I arrived at that big office building, I was hustled through to the meeting room where I was going to be sharing an hour or so with Caleb Teller. He was the one running the meetings. Violet had told me before she had kicked my ass out the door. He was the boss too, so I should make sure I kept him on my good side.

"Great to meet you," I told him warmly, trying to keep the smile on my face and the nerves out of my voice.

The job was for an assistant to the boss, exactly what I had been doing with Damian. I was experienced enough to pull this off. I just had to make sure they knew that, and I could walk out of here with the job.

"You too, Lilah," Caleb replied. "You seemed really enthusiastic about this position on the phone, and we're always looking for that kind of go-getting attitude around the office."

"Of course," I said as smoothly as I could, hoping the surprise didn't register on my face.

So Violet had really gone all the way out there to impersonate me on the phone? Damn, that was further than I thought she would dare to go. I needed to talk to her about what the hell had brought this on, but for now, the most important thing was getting through the interview and making the best impression I could.

"So we took a look over your CV, and it seems like you're really well suited to the position we're recruiting for right now," he said.

I nodded. "Yes, I've had experience at similar companies before."

"I see you worked with Damian Cross for a while," he said as he skimmed over the page in front of him. Though there was an attempt at being casual in his voice, I could tell this was what he had been hoping to talk about from the start.

"Yes, that's correct."

"Can I ask?" He leaned forward, pushed the rimless glasses up his nose, and fixed me with a hard stare. "What was it that made you decide to move on? Especially considering you applied to work here with us so soon afterwards."

I hadn't considered this question, but honestly, what did I expect? I couldn't just stroll on out of a job one day and walk into another one in a similar place the next without somebody asking a few questions.

How quickly could I bullshit my way to an answer to his question?

"Working with him was very instructive," I replied. "But it became clear pretty swiftly that we weren't a good fit for one another with regards to schedule. My family lives here in the city, you see, and he travels a lot. We eventually came to the conclusion that it wasn't right for me to keep working for him when I had so much going on back here. Family commitments, things like that."

"I see," Caleb replied, and he seemed satisfied by that answer.

Thank goodness. Okay, so I had managed to talk my way out of that corner.

"So, you'd prefer more work in the city?" he asked.

I nodded. "Yes, that's what I'm hoping for," I said.

He pressed his lips together, seeming to appreciate the answer. I had no idea what I was doing here. I really felt like I was swimming through syrup and just trying to keep moving forward, but it seemed to be working so far.

"So tell me a little about your experience working with Damian," he said. "Full disclosure, as I'm sure you're aware, we had a brief involvement with his company."

"So you know him then?" I asked with curiosity.

"Yes, we know him," he replied, his face not registering a hint of emotion. "We have done business with him before, and we are aware of his status in the industry."

He seemed annoyed to have to come out and mention it at all, but I would have been lying if I wasn't intrigued to know what was going on behind the venom of that statement.

Was he jealous of Damian's success? Maybe that he came from a family that already had plenty of cash to get started with? I had no idea, but I wouldn't have been surprised if that was part of the reason I had gotten through this door.

People seemed to want the inside scoop on Damian one way or another, and as his ex-assistant, I seemed to be the go-to for getting that. Not that I had any plans to tell anyone anything, but perhaps if I teased it a little, people might be more inclined to hire me.

He asked me a little more about Damian but then moved on to the experience I'd had working for him. I had decided to skip out on mentioning the coffee shop on my new resume, figuring it would be best to skip the part where I walked out of a new job just because an old flame had wandered in.

Besides, I didn't want anyone to think I was getting into these positions because I just wanted to hook up with the rich guys. Last thing I needed around here was a reputation.

"Well, I have to say, I really like the look of your application," Caleb said once he seemed to have run out of questions.

He asked if there was anything I wanted to know about the position, and I had managed to ask a couple of questions I was pretty sure made me sound knowledgeable and smart, as opposed to groping around in the dark because my roommate had dumped me out here without letting me know she was planning it in the first place.

"We have a few more people to interview before we're done for the day, but look—let me just say this." He lowered his voice, even though it was just the two of us in the room. "Keep Monday morning free for me. I can't guarantee you anything at this point, but I think you may well be the best applicant we're going to get through the door for the time being."

"Of course," I replied, and I couldn't help but feel a little giddy. I couldn't believe it. I had woken up this morning not even knowing I had an interview at all, and now I might be walking out of here with a job. A full-blown job. A job doing what I knew I was good at. And a job somewhere I knew Damian would find out about—not that it mattered, but still, it was pleasing to know he might find out about my new position.

"Thanks for coming in today," he told me warmly as he got to his feet and stuck his hand out in my direction. "We'll be in touch. It won't be long until you hear from us again, all right?"

"All right," I replied, and I had to bite my lip to keep the huge smile from spreading over my face. I needed to play it cool. As cool as I could.

The smile that Caleb gave me as he saw me out the door was enough to tell me this had been worth rushing out of bed for.

"Thanks for meeting me," I said, and I headed for the door and marched out of the building, feeling as though I was walking on air.

Yes! Yes. Okay, I was going to have to fight the urge to punch the air and dance around the street, brushing by all the worker drones that I was totally going to be a part of soon enough. I couldn't believe how happy I was at that prospect. I couldn't believe I had actually pulled it off.

After things had gone to shit with Damian, I had convinced myself I wasn't meant for this part of the workforce. I had only gotten that job because of Melanie, after all. But now, after maybe getting this one, I knew I could make this work.

Life might not have been easy these last few weeks, but it was finally taking a turn for the better. As I walked down the street, I almost felt like dancing, kicking my heels in the air, and letting loose. I deserved it. After all this time, I deserved it. And I knew I had Violet to thank for it all.

That, of course, was the moment I laid eyes on Damian fucking Cross once more.

Chapter Twenty-Two

Damian

AS SOON AS I SAW HER, I strode toward her quickly, but she looked away from me and started to head in the other direction.

She had done an about-face turn right where she stood, so I knew this wasn't just her happening to wander off. She had seen me, and she wanted nothing to do with me.

"Lilah!" I called after her, and finally, she came to a halt and turned to face me, her expression pretty pissed. I couldn't blame her. I had turned up here out of the blue, after all. I just wanted to see if what Violet had told me was true—and by the looks of it, she had been pretty honest with me.

"Hey," she greeted me as she crossed her arms over her chest. "What are you doing here?"

"Violet told me you'd started work here," I explained to her. "I wanted to see if that was true. It seems it is."

"Well, that explains everything," she muttered.

I cocked an eyebrow at her, confused. "What do you mean?"

"I'm not working here," she replied. "At least, not yet. Violet was spinning some story. I'm not sure why. When the hell did the two of you see each other anyway?"

"Earlier this week, we ran into each other on the street," I explained, furrowing my brow. "Wait, so you're not working here? Then what are you doing at the building?"

"I'm interviewing for a job, Damian," she told me, her voice cold and annoyed. "If that's fine by you, of course. Because you can't seem to stop turning up at the places that I'm meant to be working, can you?"

"The coffee shop was a coincidence," I said.

"And this?" she replied, glaring at me. "What would you say this is? What should I put on the police report?"

I fell silent. She had a point. I had no right to be here, but I had wanted to see her. And it wasn't just about her working for this other company, though I could frame it as that, thank goodness, so she didn't get too suspicious. There was far more to it than that. Far more to it than I would have cared to admit. Far more to it than I think I wanted to speak out loud.

"Are you going to be working here?" I asked her, ignoring the question. Being this close to her, even when she was giving me that hard-ass look, made me feel alive in a way that I hadn't in far too long.

"Whenever they want me to start," she shot back. "So give up on any hope you had that I was going to come crawling back to you looking for a job. Sorry, but it's not going to happen."

"I wasn't hoping that you would," I lied sharply, my voice coming out snappier than I had intended.

I could see her start at the sound of it. Shit, this was what had landed me in this mess in the first place, my complete fucking inability to let go of the control that I craved so deeply. The fact that I needed to defend myself when there was nothing left to defend against. If I had just been a little kinder to her on the last day of that trip, I wouldn't have been in this situation.

"Well, lucky for you, because I've moved on," she told me. "By the way, you left your coat at our place. You need to come pick it up, or else I'll have to donate it to a thrift store."

She turned to walk away from me, and that was when I felt it. That sureness that I couldn't let her go.

Maybe I was being crazy. Maybe I needed to let go and move on, but there was something about the finality of what she had just said that struck a chord deep within me.

I didn't want her to leave. I didn't care if she wanted to scream and shout at me and tell me all day long that I was nothing more than a creep and an asshole who she wanted nothing to do with. I just had to be close to her.

And that meant there was no way in hell I was letting her go to work for that rival company of mine. Once they had her, they wouldn't let me near her again. She would be able to move on, and I couldn't have that, not yet, not when it felt like there was so much left unspoken between us.

"Hey, Lilah," I said.

She looked at me, eyebrows raised expectantly, annoyance written all over her face. "Can I help you?"

"You can't take that job."

She stared at me for a moment, then rolled her eyes, and shook her head.

"I'm sorry, but you don't get to decide what's good for me anymore," she replied.

"I'm not talking about what's good for you," I replied. And then, it clicked in my head. This didn't have to be something to do with the way I felt about her. This could be something to do with what had gone down when we were working together.

"Check your contract," I replied.

"What are you going on about?" she snapped back, but I could see the flicker of doubt in the back of her mind. I was getting to her. That was all I needed to see.

"The contract that you signed when you first came to work with me," I reminded her. "You read it all, right?"

"Of course, I did. I'm not an idiot."

"Then you know that there's a no-compete clause," I said. "Which says that you can't work for anyone else in the industry. You remember that, right?"

She stared at me for a long moment. She might have claimed to have read the clause, but it was pretty clear from the look on her face that she hadn't been expecting this.

"I don't know what you're talking about," she replied, but she didn't move a muscle, as though she knew this was something she had to stop and pay attention to.

"I know you don't want to hear it, but this is how it is," I told her. "You can't work for any of my competitors. I'm sure you understand that. It's just not appropriate for you to go and get involved with someone who might use whatever knowledge you gained against me. You have to understand that."

She looked like she had been slapped in the face. She chewed her lip and stared at me for another moment, as though she was waiting for me to take it all back and undo what I had just said to her. But I couldn't. I wasn't going to.

"I'm not listening to any of this," she told me, and she turned on her heel and marched away from me.

I called after her again. I wasn't letting her leave just like that. Not a chance in hell.

"You have to," I told her firmly, and she came to a halt once more.

When she looked over her shoulder at me, I could sense the anger coming off her in waves. Well, yeah, sorry, but there wasn't anything I could do about it.

I wanted to be able to let her go, but there was no way I was allowing this woman to just walk out of my life. Not after everything we had been through together. Not after everything we had experienced. I cared for her too much for anything close to that, and even as she stood there and gazed at me as though she was wondering what the hell I was raving about, I knew there was nothing I wouldn't do to keep her close.

"You're really going to do this to me?" she asked, her voice low and a little sad. Maybe she had thought better of me, but then, she had never known me in my full business mode. She didn't know what I would do to make sure everything stayed the way it was meant to.

I could pretend this was about work, but I knew it was something far more than that, something that ran far deeper, even though I wanted to pretend it was just another corner of my life I was getting under control.

"You have to find some way to get over this," she spat in my direction, and I could tell that she was on the brink of going over the edge and into something that she couldn't take back.

Maybe I deserved that. Maybe I deserved to be treated that way, to be talked to like I was nothing more than some bastard coming around to make her life worse. I had just rolled up in front of her when she had been walking out of an interview, after all, practically stalking her to this new job.

No wonder she was mad. She looked as though she could have lit me on fire with her eyes.

"It's not about us," I said, even though I knew it was a stone-cold lie. "This is about my business. I know you don't care about that, but I do, and I'm not about to let the woman who worked so closely with me stroll into some new job with someone I already know has a problem with me."

"What problem does he have with you?" she asked, a flicker of intrigue in her eyes.

I shook my head. She was crazy if she thought I was going to share that with her.

"That doesn't matter," I replied, waving my hand to dismiss the very thought of what she was saying to me. "What matters is that you made a promise to me and my company, and you're going to be breaking that if you go and work for him."

I knew I had won. I put those clauses in every single one of the contracts of anyone who worked for me, and I wasn't going to let anything change that. This was exactly why, because I knew the competitors around me liked to try and scoop up the people who were close to me, to try and undermine what I had worked so hard to achieve.

"I made a promise to you," she muttered, so quiet that the sound of the words was almost whisked away in the crowd around us.

I nodded. "You know that you did. You know this is how this works, Lilah. You can't walk into a new job after you spent all that time with me, not with a competitor, and even more so with someone who I know has an issue with me. Do you understand that?"

"You just can't let go, can you?" she replied, her eyes narrowing, a flare of fury coming off her now like she couldn't contain it anymore.

"What are you talking about?"

"Oh, don't play dumb with me. I know you better than that." She rolled her eyes. "I know what this is about. You can stand there and pretend that you don't just want to control me, but I know you, Damian. You forget that, but I know you."

"You don't know me," I shot back, more defiant than anything else. I knew it wasn't true. She knew me better than I had allowed anyone to know me in a hell of a long time.

I wanted to hide myself from her, but there was no way I could do that, not when she could look at me and see right through me to the man I had been when I had allowed myself to fall for her.

"I know you," she replied, her voice low. "I know you well enough to see right through this. You can pretend it's about work, but I know it's not. I know you just want to control me."

She took a deep breath, rolling her shoulders back and pulling herself into this power pose that seemed to scream to anyone looking that she wasn't going to take another minute of my shit.

"You need to let me live my life, Damian," she told me loudly. "You need to let me live my life and get on with everything that I want to do with it. You can't keep following me around and trying to get in my way like this. It's not okay. And I'm not going to stand for it anymore."

"The contract you signed says something different," I reminded her.

She didn't even flinch. She had been expecting me to throw that back in her face.

"I have to move on," she said. "I'm just asking you to do the same thing." She turned on her heel and marched away.

There was so much more that I wanted to say to her, so much more that I needed to come out with, so much more that I had to get her to listen to before she left me, but she wasn't going to stick around and hear another word of it.

Maybe I deserved that. And maybe she had a point. Maybe I did need to move on, to let go, to find some way to move forward among the chaos that all of this seemed to be leaving behind.

As I stood there, it took me a moment to recognize myself. Who was this man who had fallen so hard for a woman that he couldn't let her go? That he didn't want to be apart from her no matter what? Who was willing to follow her down to the location of some new job just in the hopes of catching a glimpse of her once more?

He was the same man who was willing to throw back in her face something that she had signed for me a long time ago. Something that I normally forgot I even put in my contracts. The guy who could make her look at me as though I was the biggest bane on her life that she had ever encountered. The guy who could make her walk away from him like there was nowhere she would rather be than as far from him as possible.

I only had myself to blame for all of this. I only had myself to blame for the mess I had made. I didn't know if there would ever be a way for me to make it right, but I was sure as hell going to start looking.

And that started right here, right now.

Chapter Twenty-Three

Lilah

I SLAMMED ONE OF THE balls across the range and watched it sail into the distance in front of me. That felt a little better now, didn't it?

In truth, I was just starting to feel more and more frustrated with every moment that passed. I couldn't believe he had really managed to win like that. I'd just had to turn down a perfectly good job because Damian couldn't seem to accept that I had better things to do than stick around and hope that he would take me back.

I hadn't been able to see a way around the no-compete clause in the contract for Damian, so with great regret, I'd had to go to Caleb and tell him I couldn't take the job that he had so kindly offered me. He'd looked pretty stunned when I had told him why, and I offered him yet another apology, hoping it would be enough to keep me from landing in anyone's bad books.

"This isn't how I wanted it to go," I told him. "I would never have applied at this place if I'd realized this could happen."

"No, no, it's fine," he assured me, and he shook his head. "I should have known that Damian would make sure nobody would be able to get anything past him."

I stared at him for a moment. Was Caleb seriously impressed with Damian right now? How much of a hard-on did he have for the guy that even him keeping Caleb from getting a new assistant was something that Caleb could spin into proof of how excellent he was? Damian's reputation, I was beginning to figure out, stretched further than I had ever imagined it would.

"Well, if I ever get a chance, I'll be sure to be back in touch," I promised him, but Caleb already seemed to have committed to the idea of being impressed by the fact that Damian had gotten me to do just what he wanted.

Okay, so that was pretty annoying. Maybe I should have taken it as a win and moved on, but instead, I couldn't help but feel that nagging sensation, that reminder that Damian still *owned* me in the eyes of almost everyone else in this business.

I had never responded well to that. I had never been the girl who wanted to be attached to someone else, but Damian had made it so that it was impossible for me to get away from that.

And that was why I found myself down at the driving range for the afternoon. I needed to blow off some steam, and this was the best way to do just that. My skin prickled under the heat of the sun around me, and I swung hard against the balls, sending them flying wildly across the green.

I wasn't sure anyone else was happy that I was there, but that was none of their business. If they had an issue with the way I was doing things, they would just have to suck it up and get over it.

I let out a little grunt as I sent one of the balls spinning toward the horizon, and I shielded my eyes to watch it bounce off into the distance. All this sunshine and golf made me think of Damian, and it was almost enough to get me thinking of California again.

If I wasn't really careful about where I was letting my mind wander to, I might have had that trip going round and round my head over and over again, feeling like it was never going to end, like I was never going to get a break from the way it made me feel. If I wasn't careful, of course.

The anger wasn't just directed at Damian, of course. Some of it was turned inward at myself. It wasn't going to achieve anything, but I couldn't help it. I couldn't believe I had been so stupid as to just sit back and allow all of this to happen.

I should have read that contract back to back, inside and out, before I even thought about signing. But back when I'd first gotten that job, I could never have predicted that any of this would happen. All I saw was the chance to take on some work that actually paid well when I needed it more than anything in the world. I would have signed away my soul if they'd asked me to. Hell, I hadn't read it again recently. Maybe I had done just that without knowing it.

I needed work. I needed a job. But it seemed like anywhere I tried to turn, Damian was there to make sure that my efforts were derailed one way or another. Why did he do this to me? He could have just held his hands up and let me move on, and all this could have been done with. But he just wasn't able to let go of things that easily.

It was all about control with him. It always had been. I hadn't realized just what a control freak he was until I tried to break away, and then it became clear.

I was pissed, of course, but some part of me enjoyed knowing he still held me so close and tight. That he wasn't willing to let me go just yet.

And the fact that I liked it? Well, that just made me even angrier. What the hell was wrong with me? I should have been spitting, not celebrating.

I needed to see him face to face. I needed to talk to him. To show him once and for all just what I thought of him. I wasn't going to let him throw down in my shit and get in the way of the life I was trying to live.

Paying my fee, I stormed away from the driving range. I was going straight to his office, and I was going to let that fucker know just what I thought of him. His bullshit had gone on long enough, and nobody had held him accountable for shit like he was trying to make happen right now. That wasn't right. He didn't deserve that. Everyone else had to own up to their mistakes, so why did Damian get a pass?

By the time I arrived at the office, I considered cooling myself off a little, trying to get myself to relax a bit first so I wouldn't get stressed when I saw him, but I had already shot deep into over-reaction zone. I marched up to the office, trying to ignore the strange rush of *deja vu* that ran through me as I headed to the desk where I used to work.

I knocked on his door. Without waiting for an answer, I opened it and walked inside.

"Lilah?" Damian asked, getting to his feet like he had been caught in the act. "What are you doing here?"

"We need to talk," I told him. I didn't even know what I intended to say to him, but I had to come up with something.

"About what?"

I exploded at him at last. "I turned down that job for you. I didn't take it because I didn't want to get in the way of the no-compete clause in the contract. You hear me? I gave it up for you, even though they would have taken me on in an instant."

"Yeah, seems like the right thing to do," he replied coolly. "Wouldn't want me making a fuss after you started working there, would you?"

"Not that you would have done a thing like that," I said, so angry I was having a hard time seeing straight.

He seemed amused by me turning up here. Oh, I would show him what was really funny about all of this.

"I told you," he said. "I've got to protect my interests."

I shook my head. "And why do your interests always seem to have something to do with me? Why can't you just let me get on with my life?"

"You're the one who signed the contract."

"And you're the one who wrote it in the first place," I said, not letting him slide out of that one so easily.

I hated this. I hated how being around him made me feel alive in a way I hadn't in way too long. I hated the way my skin seemed to light up when I was around him. I hated how hard my heart was beating in my chest, as though it was trying to pump right on out of my system and toward him.

"It's pretty standard practice," he said, holding his hands up. "I'm just doing what anyone else would in my situation. You can't blame me for that."

"Everyone in this town already worships you," I replied. "Why would you need to do something like that when you already know that?"

"Sounds like Caleb had some nice things to say about me," he said.

I clenched my fists at my sides and took a step toward him. "It doesn't matter what he had to say about you. Because I'm not going to be working for him anyway."

"Quite right."

"Don't talk to me like that," I said, exasperated. "Come on. You know you don't own me anymore. I'm not going to spill any state secrets. I just need a job. And I'm not going to come back and work here, especially not when you're acting like a total ass about all of this."

"That's no way to talk to someone the whole city worships," he replied, and I could tell that he was getting riled up too. It was childish but kind of a relief to see he was getting as mad as I was.

I needed to know I wasn't the only one who felt as strongly as this right now. I couldn't be. What we'd had couldn't just be dismissed or brushed away like that. It mattered and I needed to know he understood that the same way I did. Just the same way I felt it.

"Oh, you'd love that, wouldn't you?" I asked, moving closer to him. "You'd love it if everyone could just start playing by your rules. Then you would never have to even think about anyone else ever again. You could just have things the way you wanted them, and then you could run everything just the way you wanted it. Do you know how pathetic it makes you that you can't even handle the idea of anyone else doing something you don't like?"

He glared at me. "Just because I want things the way I like them—"

"It's not the way you like them," I said. "It's the way you need them, or else you just blow up at the people around you. Even when they've done nothing wrong. Even when they weren't the ones to make the mistakes in the first place, you still find some way to make a scene and cause chaos because you didn't get what you wanted. It's pathetic. You must know that."

"Nobody speaks to me like that," he warned me.

I rolled my eyes and shook my head. "You better get used to it," I replied. "Because I don't work for you anymore, and I'm going to talk to you however I want to."

"Yeah, you don't work for me," he said. "And you have yet to explain why the hell you're in my office when you have no intention of coming back here to pick up where you left off."

"Because as long as you're going to keep getting in the way of me getting an actual job," I replied. "I'm going to make myself a nuisance around yours. Get it?"

"Oh, I get it," he replied. "You can't stay away. You haven't got enough going on in your life for that."

"You don't know anything about my life," I snapped back at him.

He narrowed his eyes at me. "I know you have the time to come down here in the middle of the day and make a scene for no good reason," he shot back angrily. "You want to explain that? Because I would love to hear what you have to say for yourself."

"There's nothing I need to say," I replied. "I just wanted you to know that you're keeping me from the real world right now, and you've only got yourself to blame for it."

"You think I don't blame myself enough already?"

The veracity of his words caught me off-guard. "What are you talking about?" I asked, my voice still angry even though it had all begun to fade by then.

"I'm talking about the fact that you're standing right there in front of me and I can't hear a word you're saying because all I want to do is kiss you right now," he growled back at me.

My jaw dropped. It was the last thing I had expected to hear coming out of his mouth. But as soon as I heard him say it, I dove toward him and planted my lips against his.

I didn't know what came over me. I needed him. I needed this. This fucking asshole—I had to have him.

He wound his arms around me and pushed me down onto the desk, both of us moving so quickly that we didn't have time to think about what an obviously bad idea this was.

His hands were hot and hungry as they moved all over my body. Were we really going to do this? Right here, in his office? I didn't know, but at the same time, I couldn't stop. I wanted this. Needed this. Needed him. Had needed him from the moment I made the choice to come back to this office.

Suddenly, the door sprang open behind us, and the two of us jumped apart. I didn't know who I expected to see there in front of me, but as soon as I figured out who it was, my jaw dropped.

"Dad?" Damian demanded, straightening his shirt. "What are you—"

"What the hell do you think you're doing, stealing my business out from under me?" His father cut him off. His face was like thunder.

I had just walked into the middle of something I should never have been close to.

THE END

Delegating Love – COMING SOON

Assisting the Boss Series

Book 1 – Billion Reasons
Book 2 – Duke of Delegation
Book 3 – Late Night Meetings
Book 4 – Delegating Love
Book 5 – Suitors & Admirers

Find Lexy Timms:

LEXY TIMMS NEWSLETTER:
  http://eepurl.com/9i0vD
  Lexy Timms Facebook Page:
  https://www.facebook.com/SavingForever
  Lexy Timms Website:
  http://www.lexytimms.com

Want

FREE READS?

Sign up for Lexy Timms' newsletter
And she'll send you updates on new releases,
ARC copies of books and a whole lotta fun!

Sign up for news and updates!
http://eepurl.com/9i0vD

More by Lexy Timms:

FROM BEST SELLING AUTHOR, Lexy Timms, comes a billionaire romance that'll make you swoon and fall in love all over again.

Jamie Connors has given up on men. Despite being smart, pretty, and just slightly overweight, she's a magnet for the kind of guys that don't stay around.

Her sister's wedding is at the foreground of the family's attention. Jamie would be fine with it if her sister wasn't pressuring her to lose weight so she'll fit in the maid of honor dress, her mother would get off her case and her ex-boyfriend wasn't about to become her brother-in-law.

Determined to step out on her own, she accepts a PA position from billionaire Alex Reid. The job includes an apartment on his property and gets her out of living in her parent's basement.

Jamie must balance her life and somehow figure out how to manage her billionaire boss, without falling in love with him.

** The Boss is book 1 in the Managing the Bosses series. All your questions won't be answered in the first book. It may end on a cliff hanger.

For mature audiences only. There are adult situations, but this is a love story, NOT erotica.

Faking It Description:

HE GROANED. THIS WAS torture. Being trapped in a room with a beautiful woman was just about every man's fantasy, but he had to remember that this was just pretend.

Allyson Smith has crushed on her boss for years, but never dared to make a move. When she finds herself without a date to her brother's upcoming wedding, Allyson tells her family one innocent white lie: that she's been dating her boss. Unfortunately, her boss discovers her lie, and insists on posing as her boyfriend to escort her to the wedding.

Playboy billionaire Dane Prescott always has a new heiress on his arm, but he can't get his assistant Allyson out of his head. He's fought his attraction to her, until he gets caught up in her scheme of a fake relationship.

One passionate weekend with the boss has Allyson Smith questioning everything she believes in. Falling for a wealthy playboy like Dane is against the rules, but if she's just faking it what's the harm?

A chance meeting with one of the company photographers may turn into more than just an impromptu photo shoot.

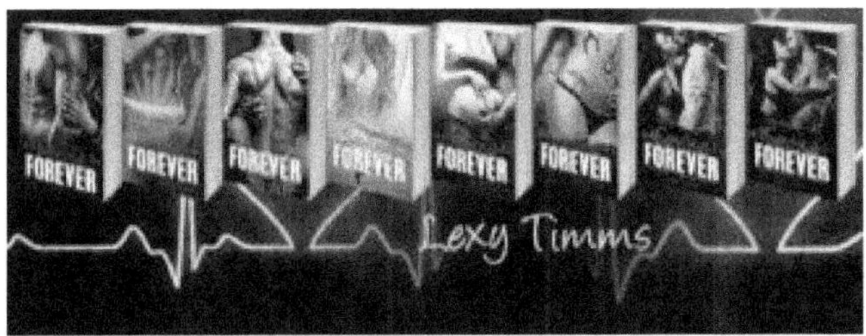

Book One is FREE!

SOMETIMES THE HEART needs a different kind of saving… find out if Charity Thompson will find a way of saving forever in this hospital setting Best-Selling Romance by Lexy Timms

Charity Thompson wants to save the world, one hospital at a time. Instead of finishing med school to become a doctor, she chooses a different path and raises money for hospitals – new wings, equipment, whatever they need. Except there is one hospital she would be happy to never set foot in again—her fathers. So of course, he hires her to create a gala for his sixty-fifth birthday. Charity can't say no. Now she is working in the one place she doesn't want to be. Except she's attracted to Dr. Elijah Bennet, the handsome playboy chief.

Will she ever prove to her father that's she's more than a med school dropout? Or will her attraction to Elijah keep her from repairing the one thing she desperately wants to fix?

THE ONE YOU CAN'T FORGET

Emily Rose Dougherty is a good Catholic girl from mythical Walkerville, CT. She had somehow managed to get herself into a heap trouble with the law, all because an ex-boyfriend has decided to make things difficult.

Luke "Spade" Wade owns a Motorcycle repair shop and is the Road Captain for Hades' Spawn MC. He's shocked when he reads in the paper that his old high school flame has been arrested. She's always been the one he couldn't forget.

Will destiny let them find each other again? Or what happens in the past, best left for the history books?

** *This is book 1 of the Hades' Spawn MC Series. All your questions may not be answered in the first book.*

FORTUNE RIDERS MC
BILLIONAIRE BIKER
LEXY TIMMS
Download For
FREE
Lexy
Timms

MC
ONE YOU CAN'T
Forget
BESTSELLING AUTHOR
LEXY TIMMS
Lexy
Timms
Grab Your
FREE
Copy Today!

A Burning Love Series

Book 1 – Spark of Passion
Book 2 – Flame of Desire
Book 3 – Blaze of Ecstasy

A Maybe Series

Book 1 – Maybe I Should
Book 2 – Maybe I Shouldn't
Book 3 – Maybe I Did

Don't miss out!

Visit the website below and you can sign up to receive emails whenever Lexy Timms publishes a new book. There's no charge and no obligation.

https://books2read.com/r/B-A-NNL-LMTEB

BOOKS 2 READ

Connecting independent readers to independent writers.

Did you love *Late Night Meetings*? Then you should read *Her Body-guard*[1] by Lexy Timms!

Protecting Diana is a 5 book mini series by USA Today Bestselling Author, Lexy Timms.

His security company is the hottest on the market, but that doesn't mean his job is easy.

Ethan Stark has three rules:

Never get personally involved.

Never get blindsided.

And never screw around. Ever.

His Special Forces background, coupled with his family's resources, have made him successful, but they didn't prepare him for the politi-

---

1. https://books2read.com/u/3krYyK

2. https://books2read.com/u/3krYyK

cian's daughter with a body that could make grown men weep, and an attitude that puts his teeth on edge.

He's agreed to guard her as a personal favor to her father, but he's beginning to wonder how long he can put up with her spoiled brat ways. That is, until she sets her seductive sights on him.

Now he's got to keep her safe from a mystery threat while keeping it in his pants. Sometimes he thinks facing off an entire army would be easier...

Read more at www.lexytimms.com.

Also by Lexy Timms

A Bad Boy Bullied Romance
I Hate You
I Hate You A Little Bit
I Hate You A Little Bit More

A Burning Love Series
Spark of Passion
Flame of Desire
Blaze of Ecstasy

A Chance at Forever Series
Forever Perfect
Forever Desired
Forever Together

A Dating App Series
I've Been Matched
You've Been Matched

We've Been Matched

A "Kind of" Billionaire
Taking a Risk
Safety in Numbers
Pretend You're Mine

A Maybe Series
Maybe I Should
Maybe I Shouldn't
Maybe I Did

Assisting the Boss Series
Billion Reasons
Duke of Delegation
Late Night Meetings
Delegating Love

BBW Romance Series
Capturing Her Beauty
Pursuing Her Dreams
Tracing Her Curves

Beating the Biker Series

Making Her His
Making the Break
Making of Them

Billionaire Banker Series
Banking on Him
Price of Passion
Investing in Love
Knowing Your Worth
Treasured Forever
Banking on Christmas

Billionaire Holiday Romance Series
Driving Home for Christmas
The Valentine Getaway
Cruising Love

Billionaire in Disguise Series
Facade
Illusion
Charade

Billionaire Secrets Series
The Secret
Freedom
Courage

Faking It
Temporary CEO
Caught in the Act
Never Tell A Lie
Fake Christmas
Fake Billionaire Box Set #1-3

Firehouse Romance Series
Caught in Flames
Burning With Desire
Craving the Heat
Firehouse Romance Complete Collection

Forging Billions Series
Dirty Money
Petty Cash
Payment Required

For His Pleasure
Elizabeth
Georgia
Madison

Fortune Riders MC Series
Billionaire Biker
Billionaire Ransom

Billionaire Misery

Fragile Series
Fragile Touch
Fragile Kiss
Fragile Love

Great Temptation Series
The Devil's Footsteps
Heaven's Command
Mortals Surrender

Hades' Spawn Motorcycle Club
One You Can't Forget
One That Got Away
One That Came Back
One You Never Leave
One Christmas Night
Hades' Spawn MC Complete Series

Hard Rocked Series
Rhyme
Harmony
Lyrics

Heart of Stone Series
The Protector
The Guardian
The Warrior

Heart of the Battle Series
Celtic Viking
Celtic Rune
Celtic Mann
Heart of the Battle Series Box Set

Heistdom Series
Master Thief
Goldmine
Diamond Heist
Smile For Me
Your Move
Green With Envy
Saving Money

Highlander Wolf Series
Pack Run
Pack Land
Pack Rules

How To Love A Spy
The Secret
The Secret Life
The Secret Wife

Just About Series
About Love
About Truth
About Forever

Justice Series
Seeking Justice
Finding Justice
Chasing Justice
Pursuing Justice
Justice - Complete Series

Kissed by Billions
Kissed by Passion
Kissed by Desire
Kissed by Love

Leaning Towards Trouble
Trouble

Discord
Tenacity

Love on the Sea Series
Ships Ahoy

Love You Series
Love Life
Need Love
My Love

Managing the Billionaire
Never Enough
Worth the Cost
Secret Admirers
Chasing Affection
Pressing Romance
Timeless Memories
The Night Before Christmas

Managing the Bosses Series
The Boss
The Boss Too
Who's the Boss Now
Love the Boss
I Do the Boss

Wife to the Boss
Employed by the Boss
Brother to the Boss
Senior Advisor to the Boss
Forever the Boss
Christmas With the Boss
Billionaire in Control
Billionaire Makes Millions
Billionaire at Work
Precious Little Thing
Priceless Love
Valentine Love
The Cost of Freedom
Trick or Treat
Gift for the Boss - Novella 3.5
Managing the Bosses Box Set #1-3
Managing the Bosses Novellas

Model Mayhem Series
Shameless
Modesty
Imperfection

Moment in Time
Highlander's Bride
Victorian Bride
Modern Day Bride
A Royal Bride
Forever the Bride

My Best Friend's Sister
Hometown Calling
A Perfect Moment
Thrown in Together

My Darker Side Series
Darkest Hour
Time to Stop
Against the Light

Neverending Dream Series
Neverending Dream - Part 1
Neverending Dream - Part 2
Neverending Dream - Part 3
Neverending Dream - Part 4
Neverending Dream - Part 5

Outside the Octagon
Submit
Fight
Knockout

Protecting Diana Series
Her Bodyguard

Her Defender
Her Champion
Her Protector
Her Forever

Protecting Layla Series
His Mission
His Objective
His Devotion

Racing Hearts Series
Rush
Pace
Fast

Regency Romance Series
The Duchess Scandal - Part 1
The Duchess Scandal - Part 2

Reverse Harem Series
Primals
Archaic
Unitary

RIP Series
Track the Ripper
Hunt the Ripper
Pursue the Ripper

R&S Rich and Single Series
Alex Reid
Parker

Saving Forever
Saving Forever - Part 1
Saving Forever - Part 2
Saving Forever - Part 3
Saving Forever - Part 4
Saving Forever - Part 5
Saving Forever - Part 6
Saving Forever Part 7
Saving Forever - Part 8
Saving Forever Boxset Books #1-3

Shifting Desires Series
Jungle Heat
Jungle Fever
Jungle Blaze

Sin Series
Payment for Sin
Atonement Within
Declaration of Love

Southern Romance Series
Little Love Affair
Siege of the Heart
Freedom Forever
Soldier's Fortune

Spanked Series
Passion
Playmate
Pleasure

Spelling Love Series
The Author
The Book Boyfriend
The Words of Love

Taboo Wedding Series
He Loves Me Not
With This Ring

Happily Ever After

Tattooist Series
Confession of a Tattooist
Surrender of a Tattooist
Heart of a Tattooist
Hopes & Dreams of a Tattooist

Tennessee Romance
Whisky Lullaby
Whisky Melody
Whisky Harmony

The Bad Boy Alpha Club
Battle Lines - Part 1
Battle Lines

The Brush Of Love Series
Every Night
Every Day
Every Time
Every Way
Every Touch

The Debt
The Debt: Part 1 - Damn Horse
The Debt: Complete Collection

The Fire Inside Series
Dare Me
Defy Me
Burn Me

The Gentleman's Club Series
Gambler
Player
Wager

The Golden Mail
Hot Off the Press
Extra! Extra!
Read All About It
Stop the Press
Breaking News
This Just In

The Lucky Billionaire Series
Lucky Break

Streak of Luck
Lucky in Love

The Sound of Breaking Hearts Series
Disruption
Destroy
Devoted

The University of Gatica Series
The Recruiting Trip
Faster
Higher
Stronger
Dominate
No Rush
University of Gatica - The Complete Series

T.N.T. Series
Troubled Nate Thomas - Part 1
Troubled Nate Thomas - Part 2
Troubled Nate Thomas - Part 3

Toxic Touch Series
Noxious

Undercover Series
Perfect For Me
Perfect For You
Perfect For Us

Unknown Identity Series
Unknown
Unpublished
Unexposed
Unsure
Unwritten
Unknown Identity Box Set: Books #1-3

Unlucky Series
Unlucky in Love
UnWanted
UnLoved Forever

War Torn Letters Series
My Sweetheart
My Darling
My Beloved

Wet & Wild Series

Stormy Love
Savage Love
Secure Love

Worth It Series
Worth Billions
Worth Every Cent
Worth More Than Money

You & Me - A Bad Boy Romance
Just Me
Touch Me
Kiss Me

Standalone
Wash
Loving Charity
Summer Lovin'
Love & College
Billionaire Heart
First Love
Frisky and Fun Romance Box Collection
Beating Hades' Bikers

Watch for more at www.lexytimms.com.

About the Author

"Love should be something that lasts forever, not is lost forever." Visit USA TODAY BESTSELLING AUTHOR, LEXY TIMMS https://www.facebook.com/SavingForever *Please feel free to connect with me and share your comments. I love connecting with my readers.* Sign up for news and updates and freebies - I like spoiling my readers! http://eepurl.com/9i0vD website: www.lexytimms.com Dealing in Antique Jewelry and hanging out with her awesome hubby and three kids, Lexy Timms loves writing in her free time. MANAGING THE BOSSES is a bestselling 10-part series dipping into the lives of Alex Reid and Jamie Connors. Can a secretary really fall for her billionaire boss?

Read more at www.lexytimms.com.